Love's Image

To my husband, Wally, and my daughters, Alison and Lauren. I love y'all very much.

Thanks to Ned, Angela, Samantha, Nikki, Joel, Jill, Meghann, Kevin, Jessica, Lisa, Kathy, Dan, Erica, Erik, Toni, Alison, and Joydine for such great suggestions and comments. And thanks to St. Petersburg College for providing a wonderful learning experience and the opportunity to fine-tune my craft. I'd also like to thank Susan Downs and Andrea Boeshaar for all their help in making this the best manuscript it can be.

A note from the Author:
I love to hear from my readers! You may correspond with me by writing:

Debby Mayne
Author Relations
PO Box 719
Uhrichsville, OH 44683

ISBN 1-59310-260-7

LOVE'S IMAGE

Our mission is to publish and distribute inspirational products offering exceptional value and biblical encouragement to the masses.

PRINTED IN THE U.S.A.

Or check out our Web site at www.heartsongpresents.com

one

Shannon kept her gaze focused on Armand as the nurse eased the bandage away from Shannon's cheek. Armand's eyes betrayed his attempt to hide his disappointment.

"Will that. . ." He pointed to her face and quickly turned away. "Will that scar always be there?"

Shannon's throat tightened. *Scar?* Her eyes misted as she swallowed hard. The pain in her heart was worse than the pain from the accident. She couldn't speak.

"Maybe," the nurse replied, her expression stoic. Professional. "Probably."

"That's terrible," Armand said. He looked everywhere but at Shannon. His chiseled features had taken on a sallow cast, and a shadow covered his eyes as he tilted his head forward.

Reaching for his hand, Shannon found her voice and did her best to sound cheerful. "I'm sure I'll recover. My body heals fast." She couldn't let him know her fear. Fear of losing everything she'd worked so hard to accomplish. Fear of not being in control of her life. Fear of losing him.

Armand forced a smile but never looked Shannon directly in the eye again. Her heart sank, and her veins throbbed. She knew, deep down, that this was the end for them. No matter how much he'd professed his undying love, she was now certain that her beautiful face and ability to get any modeling job she wanted were not only what had attracted Armand, they had been what kept him. Now she had scars. Ugly scars. And he couldn't see past the surface.

Shannon's modeling career had taken off so fast, she wasn't

sure if she'd gone down that path because she really wanted it or because it had been handed to her on a silver platter. Whatever the case, here she was, twenty-seven, and faced with an uncertain future because she had scars. If Armand didn't stick around, at least she'd know why. Right before the accident, he'd told her he loved her and started dropping hints about the future.

Marriage, she suddenly remembered. He'd even come right out and mentioned the word *marriage.*

Nothing had changed between them since then, except two mangled cars and a four-week stay in the hospital. And a scar.

She glanced over toward the window to avoid staring at Armand. Even the weather remained the same—a disgustingly gorgeous, sunshiny day with a few puffy white clouds hovering overhead. Why couldn't it rain? Shannon didn't have any excuse except self-pity for the sick feeling in her gut. She was alive, she had plenty of financial reserves, and her family had offered their emotional support. But Armand continued sitting there, looking past her, letting her know, without words, that he couldn't face her the way she looked now.

❧

Just as Shannon feared, three days after she returned home, a flower-delivery boy stopped by with a bouquet of two dozen red roses and a card that said Armand would regrettably be out of the country for the next month or two. Shannon blinked back the tears. She knew this was a kiss-off from the man she'd been with since their photo shoot in Nassau this time last year.

A sob threatened to escape her throat, but she sniffled and swallowed deep. There had to be a solution to this problem. There was always a solution.

Shannon would never forget the first time she'd seen

Armand. While most male models spent all their time studying their reflections in the mirror or any piece of glass they passed, Armand had grinned at her and given her his undivided attention. He'd told her he loved who she was in her heart and that her looks weren't important to him. For the first time in her life, Shannon had felt like someone truly valued her for the person she was deep down. Now she knew that was a farce; they were only words spoken by a man who made a living being beautiful himself.

When she heard the knock on the door, Shannon mechanically got up and answered it. "Oh, hi, Mom."

Her mother smiled back at her, a twenty-year-older version of herself. Perfect teeth, smooth complexion, flawlessly cut, colored, and styled hair. Too bad she'd gotten pregnant and quit the performing arts program at the community college to get married.

"Don't worry, Shannon, honey," her mother told her when she opened the refrigerator and set the soup bowl on the top shelf. She turned around, glanced at Shannon, then looked everywhere but directly at her daughter. "Those cuts will heal, and you'll be back in front of the camera in no time." She'd grabbed a dishrag and started wiping down counters—a move, Shannon knew, meant to avoid looking at her.

"I don't think so, Mom," Shannon said. "These aren't just cuts. They're scars that'll be with me forever."

With a shrug and a slight grimace as they locked gazes for a split second, her mom replied, patting her on the hand, "Well, there's always plastic surgery." The lilt in her voice was a little too rehearsed. "You do what you have to do to please your fans."

Please her fans? Hardly. More like give her mother what she'd always wanted for herself—a career centered on the spotlight and superficial beauty. Bitter feelings left over from

Shannon's youth were starting to surface, and she didn't like it, so she turned to her mother and did what she'd always done. She offered a megawatt smile and got one in return.

As soon as her mother left her apartment, Shannon stood in front of her mirror, the light shining brightly on her face. For the first time since the car wreck, she took a good look at reality, really studied the damage. The windshield had gashed her when the oncoming SUV had come within inches of her face. A bright red scar started at the top of her left cheekbone and continued to the bottom of her chin. She knew if the impact had been the slightest bit stronger, she wouldn't be alive today. So why did she feel so miserable instead of grateful?

The phone rang, jolting her from the mirror and her self-pity.

"In the mood for company?"

It was Janie, the one person in her life Shannon felt certain didn't care about her looks.

"Not really."

"You don't sound so good."

"I'm fine."

"No, you're not. You shouldn't be alone right now. I'm coming over."

"You don't have to," Shannon said.

"I know I don't have to, silly. But I want to. What are friends for?"

Shannon felt a little better as she replaced the phone in the cradle. Janie had been her closest buddy back in high school, back before Shannon McNab had become a household name among the fashion conscious, TV producers, and magazine executives. Janie couldn't have cared less what Shannon did for a living or how many times her picture had been on the covers of magazines. In fact, she hated the spotlight, which worked well in their relationship, because Shannon was always the one who had it, not her.

The only thing about Janie that bothered Shannon was the fact that she liked to talk about God and her relationship with Jesus. Sometimes she spoke as if she wanted to convert Shannon. It wasn't that Shannon didn't believe in God or anything. She just didn't need religion right now. Maybe later, when she was a little older.

"Hey, Scarface."

Shannon opened the door to a grinning Janie.

With a groan, Shannon said, "I thought you wanted to make me feel better."

"Sorry. I was trying to lighten things up."

"I know. Want some soup?"

Janie chuckled. "Did Sara cook her famous chicken noodle soup? She's such a *mom*."

"Of course. Isn't that what she does every time someone gets sick?"

Janie took a step back and glared at Shannon—without the flinch or grimace Shannon was starting to expect. "You're not sick."

Okay, so Janie wasn't going to feel sorry for her. "You didn't answer me. Want some soup?"

"Sounds good." Without hesitating, Janie headed toward the kitchen and opened the refrigerator where the big glass bowl of soup sat on the top shelf. "This it?"

Shannon nodded and sank down on the vinyl kitchen chair as Janie dumped the contents of the bowl into a saucepan and set it on the front burner. She joined Shannon while the soup heated.

"Are you totally bummed about Armand?" Janie asked. She'd never minced words.

Shannon nodded then shrugged. "I guess, sort of."

"If he leaves you just because of a stupid scar, he's not worth having."

"I'm sure he had other reasons," Shannon argued. "Armand's not that shallow."

"Other reasons?" Sarcasm laced her words as Janie held up her hand and counted off on her fingers. "Let's see. You're still strikingly beautiful, even though you have that red line on your face that will probably, given time, fade to practically nothing. You're one of the sweetest people I've ever known in my life," she said as she pointed to her second finger. "Then there's the fact that you were class salutatorian, and you're smart as a whip. I guess your love of animals doesn't count since he's allergic to them." She shrugged. "Perfect woman in my book."

In spite of the pain in her heart, Shannon smiled. Janie always did have a way of putting things into perspective and bringing the positive to light. "You forgot to mention that I make a mean German chocolate cake," Shannon added, trying to get into the spirit of things and pretend none of this really mattered.

"Yeah, but you never ate any of it," Janie reminded her. "Always trying to keep those pounds off your skinny hips."

"My hips are not skinny," Shannon argued.

"Oh, come on. They are, too."

"The camera adds—"

"I know, I know," Janie interrupted. "The camera adds ten pounds. But who cares?"

"I do," Shannon said. "Well, at least I did until now."

Janie reached over and covered Shannon's hand in hers. "Maybe now you can do something you really want to do, Shannon. You never really liked modeling."

"I liked it."

Janie didn't reply to that comment, but a pensive look washed over her face as she stood. The soup had started bubbling on the stove, so she went to scoop some for both of them.

As the two of them ate the chicken noodle soup in silence, Shannon felt the comfort of sitting here with her die-hard best friend, knowing that her life was about to go in a completely different direction. She wished she could predict where it was headed, but she knew she couldn't. Nothing had prepared her for this.

"I've got a friend who just started vet assistant training," Janie blurted, interrupting Shannon's thoughts.

"What?"

"Vet assistant training," Janie repeated. "You know. Learning how to work in a veterinary office."

"Interesting."

"You might think about it, Shannon. Seriously. You love animals." She paused. "Or you can do something else."

"I don't have to do anything for a while. I have plenty of money."

"No surprise," Janie said. "But somehow I can't see you sitting back, doing nothing."

"I can read books."

"Then what?"

"Who knows? Maybe Armand will send for me."

Janie licked the soup off her lips and put down her spoon. She looked down at the table before she glanced up and locked gazes with Shannon.

"Look, sweetie, I know how hard this is for you to face, but you can't wait around for some guy to come crawling back when it's not even likely in the first place."

Shannon didn't feel like arguing. She knew how Janie felt about the whole modeling industry. At first she'd been happy for her, but after the first year, she'd told Shannon she didn't like the changes she'd seen in her.

"I haven't changed," Shannon had told her.

"You have but you just don't see it," Janie had said sadly. The whole conversation popped into Shannon's mind, and she remembered it word for word, as she often did when things became too quiet.

Shannon put down her soup spoon and leaned back. "Do you still think I've changed?" she asked.

Janie inhaled deeply as if she needed time to gather her thoughts. "Do you want the truth?"

Shannon nodded.

"You've changed in so many ways, I'm not sure where to start."

"Do you not like me anymore?"

Even if the truth hurt, Shannon needed to hear it. This was the time when she had to know what people were thinking.

"I like you, Shannon. But you used to be so much fun. You loved hiking, talking on the phone for hours on end, and acting silly with the girls. Now all you do is worry about what people think."

Shannon thought for a moment. "That's important in my business."

"But in the big scheme of things, how important is it, really?"

Janie had a point.

"I guess not very."

"My sentiments exactly."

"So what now?"

"You have to decide. Maybe you can kick back for a few weeks and read. Armand might even surprise us and call for you; I don't know. But is that what you really want, Shannon?"

"I thought it was."

"Do you want the constant threat of losing Armand just because he can't deal with the slightest imperfection? Think about it some more," Janie said as she pushed her chair back and stood. "In the meantime, I have to get back to the nursing home. Mrs. Willis needs therapy this afternoon."

They said their good-byes before Janie left. Shannon sank back on the sofa and picked up the remote control, flipping through the channels. Nothing good was on, so she turned it off. Fear clutched her chest.

What if Janie was right, and Armand didn't call?

❧

After a week went by and she still hadn't heard from Armand, Shannon knew. How could she have been fooled so easily by someone she thought loved her for her heart? He'd told her all that, hadn't he? Why would a little scar change that?

Shannon could understand why even the slightest scar would affect her modeling career. After all, she was promoting the impossible—perfect beauty, something almost every woman aspired to. But true love was blind—at least that's what she'd always thought.

"Want me to come over?" Janie asked during one of her daily phone calls. "You don't need to be alone right now."

"No, I'm fine," Shannon tried to assure her friend. "Really, I am."

"You're still in denial. What are you doing now?"

"Watching television." Which was what she'd been doing all day every day since she'd been home from the hospital.

"That's not good, Shannon. You hate TV."

Janie remembered. All her life, Shannon had been active. She played sports, hung out with friends, and stayed busy. She never had time or the inclination to sit around and watch TV. Until now.

"Look, Shannon, I'll be there in a few minutes. We'll figure something out."

"Okay."

She couldn't keep putting Janie off just because she made

her face reality. Shannon's voice had suddenly become squeaky and meek. For the first time in her life, Shannon had no idea what tomorrow would bring, and she let fear take over.

Janie was at her door less than half an hour later.

"I don't like this a single bit."

"Well, hello to you, too," Shannon said with a smirk.

"You've gotta get outta here. This place will close in on you if you don't."

"I'm fine."

"Stop saying that. No, you're not." Janie took her by the arm and gently shoved her toward the front door. "Where's your purse? I'm taking you out."

Instinctively, Shannon ran her fingertips along her cheek. Her insides lurched at the thought of people seeing her like this.

"I can't go out."

"Oh, get over it, Shannon. The sooner you face people the better. Staying inside, cooped up, hiding, won't solve any problems."

Shannon numbly let Janie guide her toward her car. Fear clutched her once again as she thought of riding in a car. "I can't."

"You can and you will." Janie held the door and nodded for Shannon to get in.

They were both buckled in the front seat of Janie's car when Shannon spoke again. "This is so silly. I'm really not in the mood."

"At the rate you're going, you'll never be in the mood."

Shannon looked out the window before turning back to face Janie, who seemed determined not to listen. "Where are we going?"

"Church." Janie put the car in reverse and carefully backed out of the parking space. "I'll be super careful. I know how hard it is to get back in a car after an accident."

Shannon remembered when Janie had hit a car head-on seven years ago. It took three strong friends to get her to ride in a car after that.

"Church?" she asked. "It's Monday. What church is open on Monday?"

"It's my singles' group."

Shannon tilted her head back and chuckled. "You go to a singles' club at a church? Now I've heard everything."

"I didn't say singles' *club*. That's for desperate people. This is my church singles' group."

"What's the difference?"

They were stopped at a red light, which gave Janie a chance to turn and face Shannon while she explained. "We discuss issues in the Bible that relate to things single people have to face today."

"Hmm."

"Yeah, hmm." Janie grinned. "This is what normal, Christ-loving people do in Atlanta. I know it sounds strange after your jet-set modeling career, but it's really nice. I think once you get into it, you might actually enjoy it."

"How long have you been doing this singles' thing at your church?" Shannon asked. This was the first she'd heard of it, although she did remember something Janie had said a couple years ago about how her life had turned completely around now that she'd let the Lord into her life. Not being one who needed that sort of thing, Shannon had glossed over it and changed the subject as quickly as she could. Now that she was being held captive, she was curious about what she was about to face.

"The singles' group started up about a year ago, and I'm one of the founding members."

Shannon shook her head. "Did you tell them about some of your shenanigans back in high school?"

"They know I'm not perfect."

Janie turned into the parking lot of a small building that looked like a converted house. Shannon looked from left to right then back at Janie.

"Where's the church?"

"We're there."

Pointing to the building, Shannon said, "This is a church? Sure doesn't look like one."

"A lot of things aren't what they look like. You should know that." She put the car in park, turned off the ignition, and opened her car door. "Let's go. Everyone will be here soon, and we start in a few minutes."

Shannon followed her friend into the building, trailing close behind. She'd always been the one eager for new experiences, but this was different. This was scary. This was church. A foreign place to Shannon.

"Hey, Janie," said a deep, masculine voice from a dark corner.

"Paul, I'm glad you're here. I have someone I want you to meet."

Suddenly, the man materialized from out of nowhere. In the semidarkness, Shannon saw him reach over and flip a switch on the wall. Light filled the space and illuminated chairs, positioned in a full circle around the room.

"Paul, this is my friend Shannon," Janie said softly.

When Shannon looked him in the eye, she saw his gaze dart to her scar. She started to lift her hand to her cheek, but he reached for her arm. "Don't," he said. "Janie told us what happened."

Shannon pulled away and looked down, letting her long, straight blond hair fall in front of her face. She'd never hidden behind her hair before, but then she'd never been scarred before either.

Instead of making a big deal of her reaction, Paul turned

his attention to Janie. "Did you talk to Jason or Dana?"

"They'll be here, but Dana said she might be late."

"That's okay. I just finished making the coffee. It's her turn to bring cookies."

Janie turned to Shannon and explained how they took turns bringing treats for the group. Shannon only half listened. Her shame was blocking her senses.

Within a couple minutes, people began to arrive, some alone and others in pairs. Fifteen minutes later, the room was filled with twenty- and thirtysomething people, all of them laughing and greeting each other as if they'd known everyone all their lives. Shannon felt ill at ease. She was perfectly comfortable at black-tie affairs where she was able to show off the latest elaborate gown some designer had created for the occasion. But this was real. She wasn't in costume. These people could see her for who she really was.

"Hey," Janie said as she walked up behind Shannon. "Lighten up. I've never seen you so shy before. You were always the life of every party."

"That was before—" She cut herself off as she reached up to touch her face again.

Janie leveled her with a stern look. "Look, Shannon, no one here cares about your scar, other than the pain you must be feeling. They don't see the scar when they look at you."

"Hey, you're that model in the corn chip ads, aren't you?"

She heard Janie groan.

Shannon whipped around and saw the man as he walked up, grinning ear-to-ear, like he'd just discovered gold. He was nice-looking but not devastatingly handsome. What she liked about him right away, though, was the way his eyes seemed to twinkle when he smiled. Like stars.

"Yeah, so she sells corn chips," Janie said before Shannon had a chance to speak. "Don't hold it against her."

The man chuckled, showing teeth with character—not perfectly straight like Armand's. But still, there was something that compelled her to continue studying him. He was interesting-looking, the corners of his lips slightly upturned, and he gazed right at her, not past her.

"What brings a famous model to our church in downtown Atlanta?" he asked.

"My friend Janie brought me," Shannon said, taking his comment at face value.

"Janie has always been full of surprises. C'mon, let's go grab some coffee before the rest of the vultures arrive."

She glanced at Janie, who'd already turned to grab a stack of Bibles from the table behind them. Shannon realized she was on her own.

Shannon followed the man to the long row of tables lined up against the wall. "I'm terribly sorry, but I didn't catch your name."

The man stopped and pivoted to face her, thrusting his right hand toward her. "Sorry. My name's Judd Manning. I'm the pastor's nephew, so I didn't exactly have a choice but to join this singles' group when I came to stay with him a few months ago." He laughed as if he knew a joke he wasn't telling. "These goons seem to think I might know something. Don't tell them my secret, but I'm just as lost as the rest of them." He made a face before adding, "Maybe even more so."

Shannon instantly felt at ease by this very nice man who became handsomer the longer they chatted. Taking his hand in hers, she tilted her head toward him. "I'm Shannon McNab."

"Yes," he said quickly. "I know."

"You know my name?"

"Uh, yeah. It's not like your picture isn't plastered all over the place."

"I guess being a model has a few drawbacks."

"You don't like it?" he asked, pulling his hand back and once again edging toward the tables.

Shannon shrugged. "Oh, I like it all right. It's just that. . ." Her hand went up to touch her face. Janie shot her a warning look, so she jerked it back down to her side.

Judd studied her face, his eyes resting on her scar, the smile fading from his lips. "What happened?"

"I thought Janie told everyone," Shannon replied.

He shrugged. "I wasn't here when Janie announced the details. I had to go out of town."

Although Shannon hated talking about it, Judd's openness made it easy for her to reply. "Car accident."

"Man, that's rough. How are you otherwise?"

"Fine, I guess."

"You're fortunate, then. It could have been much worse."

Obviously, Judd Manning didn't know what he was talking about. How could it have been any worse than it was? Did he realize she was scarred for life and would never be able to earn a living doing the only thing she knew how to do?

two

"Who wants to lead the prayer tonight?" Paul asked as he scanned the room. "Janie?"

"Sure," she replied.

Shannon listened to her best friend as she thanked the Lord for the many blessings, asked for guidance in the Bible study, and begged forgiveness for sin. The prayer wasn't long, but Shannon could tell it was heartfelt.

When everyone opened their eyes, Shannon noticed several of them looking at her, smiling. She started to reach up and cover her face, but she remembered what Janie had said. She resisted the urge and shyly grinned back.

"Janie, why don't you introduce your guest?" Paul said.

"Everyone, this is Shannon McNab. She and I have been best friends practically since we could talk," Janie began.

Judd interrupted. "And you haven't stopped talking since."

Janie shot him a glare, then continued. "Several weeks ago, Shannon had the misfortune to be in a really bad car crash. The man driving the other vehicle wasn't as fortunate, and he didn't make it. We need to pray for his family."

Shannon gulped. It hadn't crossed her mind to pray for that man's family until now. After all, the accident had been his fault. If he hadn't been drinking, she wouldn't be sitting here right now feeling like the world was staring at her scar.

"How long will you be in Atlanta, Shannon?" Paul asked.

"I, uh. . .I'm really not sure," Shannon said. She hated being put on the spot. "Probably until my—"

Janie cut in. "She's got to figure out what to do with the

rest of her life now that she won't be modeling anymore."

Shannon had never told Janie she wasn't going to model anymore. That was just an assumption she had based on her own ideas of what she thought Shannon should decide.

Hoping to end the conversation as quickly as possible, Shannon just smiled and nodded, fully intending to talk to her friend about this later—to set her straight. At some point, she needed to start speaking for herself, something she always did whenever Janie wasn't around.

As the group settled into their discussion of the scripture topic of the evening, Shannon felt the warmth of Judd's stares. She'd gotten used to people looking at her, but this was different. He never looked away when her gaze met his. He only smiled and occasionally winked. She felt her cheeks grow hot each time.

When Paul called a break, everyone stood and made a beeline for the snack table, including Janie. Out of habit, Shannon hung back. She'd learned early on that munching on snacks wasn't conducive to keeping her model figure.

"Not hungry?" Judd asked as he joined her.

She shrugged. "Not really. I don't generally eat anything after dinner."

"Which consists of a salad without dressing and water to drink, right?" He leaned away from her, studying her face, making her squirm.

She held her breath. Was he testing her?

"Whatever gave you that idea?"

"Well, isn't that what models eat? Rabbit food?"

Shannon started to argue with him, but she stopped short. What was the point? He obviously understood her as well as he possibly could, considering they'd just met. Besides, she didn't owe him anything—certainly not an explanation as to why she wasn't gorging at the snack table.

"Not exactly," she said. "But close enough."

"Yeah, I try to stay away from the desserts myself. I have to watch my figure, too." He quirked his eyebrows as she snapped around to look at him.

A retort started to form in her mind, until she realized he was having fun and kidding around with her. *Okay, time to lighten up.* She tilted her head back and forced a hearty laugh. "You're too much, Judd."

"Too much of a good thing, I hope." He suddenly looked serious, and his voice was laced with hope.

She felt a quick flash of satisfaction.

"Oh, I'm sure," she said with a little flirty hair toss. This felt really odd for Shannon. She hadn't flirted since before she'd met Armand. Who was this guy, other than some man with nothing better to do than hang out at a church on a Monday night?

"Good," he said with a self-satisfied smirk. "I'm glad you agree. I like you, too, Shannon McNab. You're not half bad for a beauty queen."

"Wait a minute." Shannon felt her defenses rise. "What, exactly, do you mean by that?"

"What I mean is," he said very slowly, drawing closer to her and lowering his voice to where no one else could hear him but her, "you're a very sweet woman. Unpretentious. Smart. Not what I'd expect from a world-class model."

His backdoor compliment caught her off guard. Her face heated once again, and her senses were out of balance. She couldn't think of a quick comeback, so she flashed one of her famous smiles. "Wow," he said. "Now I know what it's like to experience my own personal sunshine."

Most people had the wrong idea about models. They had no idea who she was deep down. Nearly everyone thought that with her looks, she could have everything she wanted with a snap of her fingers, but that simply wasn't true. Sure, Shannon was satisfied with her life for the most part, but the reality of losing it all just as quickly—as her accident had proven—was stressful.

"I have a feeling—" he began.

"C'mon, everyone," Paul said to the group, interrupting Judd. "We have a lot to cover tonight, so let's get going. Bring your coffee and cookies with you, and we'll get back to our topic."

"You have a feeling. . . ?" Shannon prompted Judd as they turned back toward the circle of chairs.

"We'll talk later," he said as he turned his attention to the speaker.

Throughout the remainder of the evening, Shannon was fully aware of the effect Judd was having on her. Each time he looked at her and smiled, she felt a tingle coursing through her. Sometimes she smiled back, but other times she tried to pretend not to notice.

After an hour, Paul requested another prayer. "Why don't you say the closing prayer, Judd?"

"You sure you want me to do this?" Judd asked.

"Yeah, but try to keep it sane, okay?"

A few snickers could be heard through the room, but Judd began his prayer. As Shannon listened to his simple words, she realized they were open, honest, and sincere.

She liked Judd Manning. He was a different kind of guy from anyone she'd ever met, but he made her feel good on the inside. She had a feeling he might be attracted to her because of who she was or how she once looked, but that wouldn't be what determined their friendship. There was nothing pretentious about him. His face wasn't perfectly chiseled like Armand's, but he was handsome enough—in a sort of scholarly way. He wore glasses and dressed in khaki slacks and a polo shirt. Nothing out of the ordinary. But he'd struck a chord in her that made her want to know more about him. The warmth of his brown eyes offered her a sense of peace and understanding.

Shannon wasn't surprised when Judd cornered her immediately after everyone stood to leave. "How long will you be in town?" he asked.

"I'm not really sure yet. Everything's still up in the air at the moment."

He studied her scar. "Tough break on the car crash, but you're still just as beautiful as ever. More beautiful, if that's possible."

Shannon chuckled. "You're too kind." She wasn't able to keep the sarcasm out of her voice.

"Really," he said as he folded his arms. "The scar gives you character."

"Character?"

"Yeah." A slow grin crept across his lips. "Perfection isn't nearly as interesting as a little flaw here and there. It shows something—"

Shannon was waiting to hear what it showed, but Janie came up and grabbed her arm. "We gotta go, Shannon. I need to drop you off and get home."

Judd tipped an imaginary hat. "Nice meeting you, Shannon McNab. Maybe I'll see you again."

"Here's her number," Janie said as she thrust a small slip of paper toward him. "Call her later."

On their way out the door, Shannon crinkled her forehead and glared at Janie. "Why'd you do that?"

"What?"

"Give him my number. I don't generally make a habit of giving my phone number out to strangers."

Janie tilted her head forward and glared at Shannon from

beneath her thick eyebrows. "Judd Manning isn't exactly a stranger, although I have to admit he can get strange at times."

"You're avoiding the point," Shannon said.

"Look, Shannon. This group is tight. If you want them to accept you as an individual and not a celebrity, you have to act like the rest of us. We exchange phone numbers." She paused before adding, "That's just something we do."

"Oh."

Once again, Shannon was given something else to think about. She'd never considered herself a celebrity, although she'd stopped giving out her number several years ago for personal reasons. Stalkers had begun invading her modeling friends' personal space, and her name was becoming known to the extent that she needed to guard a piece of her personal life. Only after getting to know someone well would Shannon give out her phone number, and even then she was nervous about it.

"Besides," Janie continued, "these people couldn't care less about what you do for a living. They're there to study the Bible."

"Is that why Judd's there? He didn't seem all that well versed—at least not as much as the rest of you."

Janie laughed. "Judd's a different subject entirely. His uncle's the pastor, so he's sort of been pushed into the group."

"He's not a Christian?"

"Oh, he's a Christian, but he admits he doesn't know scripture. We're working on him."

Shannon smiled. "He acted like he enjoyed being there."

"Judd Manning loves an audience, in case you haven't noticed. He's a clown. Everything's a joke to him."

The more Shannon heard, the more she wanted to know Judd Manning. What an interesting man.

"I like jokes," Shannon said.

With a snicker, Janie shook her head. "Yeah, but it gets old after a while." She hesitated before saying, "We still love him, though. Deep down, he's a terrific guy."

They rode in silence to Shannon's apartment. After a quick good-bye, Janie drove off, and Shannon let herself into her apartment, flipping on lights as she headed back to her bedroom.

She'd just slipped out of her shoes and into some slippers when the phone rang. She recognized the voice as Judd's even before he identified himself.

"Look, I know this is quick, but I don't believe in wasting time," he said. "Wanna get together for coffee soon?"

"Sure."

Shannon couldn't help but compare him to other guys she knew. Armand had watched her from a distance for nearly a month before he'd called the first time. She'd been aware of his gaze, so she hadn't been surprised when she'd finally heard from him. This call from Judd, on the other hand, had been completely unexpected—and very quick.

"What?"

"I'd like that."

"Cool. I wasn't sure I heard right."

"Well, you did."

"Good. How about tomorrow?"

"Okay."

"Want me to pick you up, or should we meet somewhere?"

Shannon swallowed hard. She'd always been so careful not to give out her address to people she didn't know well, but she still hadn't summoned the courage to drive, although her bright and shiny new sports car was sitting in the apartment complex parking lot, waiting for her.

"Shannon?" he said. "You still there?"

"Oh, yes, of course. Would you mind picking me up? I'm still a little skittish from the accident."

Janie knew Judd, and the worst thing she'd heard about him was that he was a clown. Where was the harm in that? Besides, he was the pastor's nephew, so he was accountable to someone respectable.

"No problem. I was thinking we could do a little catching up on the Bible study. In case you haven't noticed, I'm pretty lost in there. Those people are way ahead of me."

Shannon laughed. "I know what you mean. I feel so inadequate among all those Bible scholars."

"I don't think they'd want you to feel that way. They're a great group of people, and they'd never want to make anyone feel inadequate."

Shannon felt like she needed to backpedal. "No, that's not what I meant. I should have simply said that I felt lost and let it go."

"I know what you mean. That's why I wanted to get together with you. We can try to catch up."

Shannon's heart did a quick thud. She was surprised at her reaction of disappointment that Judd only wanted to get together with her to study and not because he was attracted to her.

"Okay, give me your address, and I'll pick you up at eight in the morning," he said, taking control.

"Eight?" She sniffled. "In the morning?"

"Yeah, unless that's too early for you. If you want to sleep in, I can make it later."

"No, no, that's okay. Eight'll be fine."

Shannon hadn't awakened before noon in years unless she had an early-morning shoot on an outdoor set. She'd have to set her alarm and do whatever it took to go to sleep at a decent time.

Strangely, she'd been very attracted to Judd and became even more so by the minute. She closed her eyes to bring his image to mind. His constantly changing expressions made him interesting to watch. One minute his forehead and the corners of his eyes crinkled with humor, and the next minute he had a pensive look on his face as the subject changed. She'd watched him throughout the Bible study, and she was intrigued by what she saw. Talking to him over the phone enhanced her desire to see him again.

❧

Judd couldn't believe he actually had a coffee date with Shannon McNab. What was he thinking? This woman was definitely out of his league.

To top it off, she'd accepted without hesitation. He swelled his chest. Maybe he wasn't such a nerd, after all.

Being the son of a military officer, Judd had moved every couple of years. Just when he'd gotten used to a place and started making friends, he'd been uprooted again. Eventually, he quit trying so hard to fit in and worked on being funny. People around him enjoyed his antics, and he didn't miss many party invitations—but he used humor to distance himself. Holding people at arms' length was his only defense in relationships.

Judd had started working for the Department of Defense, teaching in military dependent schools right after college, and he'd transferred to wherever he was needed. He had a heart for military dependents because he knew what it was like to constantly be uprooted, and he could relate to the kids. However, after teaching three years in Japan and two years in Germany, with various other short-term assignments in between, he decided to pick a spot to settle.

He'd spent quite a bit of time with his aunt and uncle in Atlanta. He loved the soft vibrancy of the southern city, so he applied for a job in a Christian school near Atlanta to finish out a vacancy left by a teacher on maternity leave. To his surprise and delight, they'd called him in right away. After the teacher's baby had arrived, she'd decided not to return, so the permanent position had been offered to Judd. Naturally, he'd accepted. As soon as summer break was over, he'd have next year's batch of lively seventh graders, some eager and others squirming over the idea of having to learn another year of language arts.

Since Uncle Garrett and Aunt LaRita had a spare bedroom after their own children had grown up and moved out, they'd offered him a place to stay until he had enough saved to buy his own house. However, there was one condition to hanging out with his favorite uncle, who happened to be a pastor—Judd had to attend weekly services and get involved in church activities. That was okay, though. Judd needed to meet and get to know people his age. Besides, he was a Christian, even though his own parents hadn't made their faith as much a part of their lives as Uncle Garrett had.

His excitement about seeing Shannon had rendered him sleepless. He went to bed early, after making plans with Shannon, so he'd be refreshed and bright in the morning.

Tossing and twisting in the sheets, trying to get comfortable, Judd couldn't still his heart. Finally, he gave up trying. He flipped on the light switch and picked up his Bible. Might as well make use of the time rather than flop around like a fish.

He reread Ephesians chapter two, verses eight and nine, the verses they'd discussed in the Bible study. "By grace are ye saved through faith; and that not of yourselves: it is the gift of God: not of works, lest any man should boast."

Faith. What a simple word. But it meant so much when he thought about it. For years, he hadn't given his faith much thought. The extent of Judd's churchgoing had been on Christmas and Easter, and even then his mind had been on the celebration afterward and not on the message.

Staying with Uncle Garrett had been an eye-opener for Judd. Uncle Garrett and Aunt LaRita started each day with a prayer, never began a meal without a blessing, and literally stopped in their tracks to close their eyes and say a prayer throughout the day. At night, before he padded to his own room, he could hear more whispered prayers coming from behind the closed door of his aunt and uncle. Those two were truly steeped in their faith.

When he'd asked Uncle Garrett if he was always happy, he'd been surprised when his question was returned with a solemn stare, then the words he hadn't expected.

"No, Judd, I can't honestly say I'm always happy. But happiness isn't my goal in life. If you think about it, happiness is a very fleeting thing. When LaRita puts a good meal down in front of me, I'm happy. But when she's away or I have to fend for myself, I'm rarely happy with what I have to eat. Last year, when I bought a new car, I was very happy, but before that, when I got the bill from the mechanic to fix my old car, I was not happy at all."

Judd had thought about what his uncle was saying and nodded. "Yeah, I see what you mean. But you always *seem* happy."

Uncle Garrett smiled. "You might be getting contentedness confused with happiness. I'm quite contented with my life because I know I'm walking close with Jesus."

That simple statement was enough to arouse Judd's curiosity. He listened more attentively to sermons now, and he did his best to understand scripture. There were times when he got lost, and he was afraid to ask others in the Bible study group. Maybe with a study partner, he'd be able to find some of the answers he'd been seeking.

Or maybe her beauty would divert his attention.

Judd sensed a restlessness in Shannon, and he couldn't put his finger on the cause. She paid close attention as everyone spoke about the lesson they'd read. Although he'd read it, he was still slightly confused, so he fell back to his clown nature.

There were times when he wondered if he had anyone fooled. The only one in the group who didn't always laugh was Shannon's friend Janie, and he sometimes thought she might actually pity him. He hoped that wasn't the case. Judd Manning wasn't to be pitied, even if he was taking baby steps in his Christian walk. He was a proud man, and the thought of anyone feeling sorry for him was annoying.

Okay, so he'd admit, pride was one of his flaws. If he could get past worrying about what people thought about him, he might be able to ask some questions and get the answers that continued to gnaw at him.

He read the same scripture lesson over and over, going back and forth between his Bible and the workbook the group was using. He underlined text and pondered it, worrying that he might be missing something.

Finally, his eyelids grew heavy. After closing both books, he said a brief prayer and turned off the light.

❧

Shannon must have tried on three different outfits before she found the right one. This was so not like her.

The first thing she'd put on was a black dress, but she realized that wasn't the right outfit for a morning coffee date. Did she dare call this a date? She hadn't been on a date with anyone but Armand in more than a year. And before that, she rarely went out because she was never sure why men wanted to be with her. She hated to be any man's arm decoration, and quite a bit of emphasis had been put on her looks, so she'd become jaded and cynical when it came to men's motives with her.

Although Judd had complimented her beauty, she had the feeling he would have asked her out regardless of her looks. Something about him seemed real. Vulnerable, even. Shannon liked that. It made her feel less on display and more equal in the relationship. One of the things she'd liked about Armand was his vulnerability—although now that she was apart from him, she saw that his weakness was from worrying too much about image. *Had she been the same way?*

Shannon shoved that question to the back of her mind. She hated to think she'd been as shallow as so many other people she'd known in her industry.

She settled on black cotton slacks and a soft pink knit pullover. It was a simple outfit that wouldn't demand attention. Her makeup had to be kept to a minimum, although she followed her urge to cover the bright red line streaking down the left side of her face. Even the thick cover stick didn't completely conceal the reminder that her professional modeling career was most likely over.

As usual, Shannon was ready a half hour early. Her nerves had awakened her before the sun came up, so she'd gone ahead and taken her shower. Now all she had to do was wait.

To her delight, the knock came at her door at precisely seven fifty-five. Judd was early, too.

"Wow." His face lit up the second she opened the door.

"Hi, Judd. Come on in."

"Last night, I thought you were a mirage. I can't believe you're actually going out for coffee with me. You look beautiful."

Shannon's stomach knotted. She stood there staring at Judd Manning as he cast an appreciative gaze over her. Maybe she'd been wrong about him.

three

Judd felt an instant barrier form between them as soon as he spoke to her. Her eyes had glazed over, and her smile wasn't nearly as bright as it had been last night.

"Do you like little diners, or are you the designer coffee-house type?" he asked.

She shrugged. "It really doesn't matter."

Yep, something had changed. Her emotional distance was so obvious, it was slamming.

"Tell you what. We can go to the Dunk 'n Dine this morning, and I'll treat you to the best two-ninety-nine breakfast you've ever tasted." He held the door for her as she slid into his car, then he leaned forward, hoping for some sort of reaction.

"That's fine," she said as she buckled her seat belt. No smile, nothing.

Judd ran around to the other side of the car, wishing he could start over. He must have said something, but what? That brightness was in her eyes when she opened her door to him, but she quickly put up her guard.

Once in his car, Judd started to crack a joke about the cat getting her tongue, but he decided to use a more direct approach instead. "What's wrong, Shannon? Did I say something?"

Not looking him in the eye, Shannon shook her head. "It's nothing."

He knew that wasn't the case. "Look, if I said something stupid, you need to tell me so I won't do it again. I've always been pretty bad about saying the wrong thing because I talk too much."

A smile tweaked the corners of her lips, but she still didn't meet his gaze. "Don't worry about it, okay?"

Now he was worried more than ever. Based on his experience, when women said not to worry, that was when a man needed to start groveling.

"I see you brought your Bible," he said, gesturing to what she was holding with a death grip.

"This is a Bible study, right?" Now that they were at the stop sign, she'd finally looked at him, but not with the cheerful expression he'd looked forward to all night.

"Yes, it is." He felt dejected and more than a little frustrated.

There had to be some way to bring back the woman he'd met last night. He didn't like the thought that something he'd said had cast a gloomy shadow over her, and he was certain she was pulling away from him because of something he'd said or done. Not being one to let things go, Judd decided to address the issue as soon as they arrived at their destination—before they went inside.

Once in the parking lot of the Dunk 'n Dine, Judd turned off the ignition and turned to face Shannon.

"Okay, spill it, Shannon. I'm sure I said something that's making you wish you'd stayed home, and I want to know what it is."

"No." Once again, she didn't look directly at him.

"C'mon, Shannon, I'm not into playing games."

Suddenly, as if he'd flipped a switch, she turned, daggers shooting from her eyes. "I don't play games," she hissed.

Frustration flooded Judd as he carefully pondered how to put his thoughts into words. "You can't expect a guy like me to know what's going on in your head unless you tell me what you're thinking."

Shannon pursed her lips and studied his face before turning to look away. He could tell she was contemplating something, hopefully an explanation that would let him know where he stood with her.

❧

This is silly, she told herself. *Just because he made a comment about my looks doesn't mean that's all he's thinking about.*

"Judd, you really didn't do anything wrong," she said slowly. "It's just that I've been ultrasensitive since the accident." Instinctively, her hand rose to her cheek.

He reached out and caught her wrist, freezing her movement. His touch sent an electric current up her arm, and time seemed to come to a screeching halt. She wondered if he could hear her heart pounding.

"Shannon, I understand your feelings. If I looked like you, something like this would probably bother me, too. But you have so much more going for you, that even if you didn't have a pretty face, you've got the world at your disposal."

Her doubts about his motives had just been squelched, at least for the moment. She turned to face him, allowing the warmth to flow between them once again.

"Thank you, Judd. You're a good guy."

He snickered. "That's what I keep trying to tell you. I'm glad you finally believe me."

Once inside, Judd ordered a short stack of pancakes and encouraged Shannon to do the same. She started to tell the waitress she only wanted coffee then decided she might as well splurge. What did it matter if she put on a pound or two now that she couldn't model?

"I'll have what he's having." Shannon stuck the plastic menu back between the napkin holder and ketchup bottle.

"You're full of surprises, Shannon McNab," Judd said. "So you *do* eat normal food."

"Yeah. What did you think I ate?" She remembered what he'd said earlier. "Rabbit food is in my past."

"Are you gonna be okay?" he asked.

"What are you talking about, Judd? Of course I'm gonna be okay. Why does everyone keep looking at me like they're afraid I'm about to shatter?"

"Maybe it's because you have a lost look on your face," he said softly.

"Lost?" Shannon cleared her throat as she slammed her Bible on the table. "I think we need to change the subject. I don't like where this is headed."

"I'm with you," Judd agreed. He began flipping the pages of his workbook. "Now where were we?"

Pointing to the workbook, Shannon asked, "Where can I get one of those? Do I have to order it?"

"I think my uncle might have some in the storage room behind his office. I'll ask this afternoon when he comes home." Judd met her gaze and turned the workbook around where they could both see it. "In the meantime, I'll share."

Once they got into the lesson, Shannon was surprised at how many answers Judd had left blank. "I thought you were the pastor's nephew. You should know these things."

Judd tilted his head back and laughed out loud. "A lot of people are disappointed to find out how little I actually know."

"I didn't say that, did I?"

"In a roundabout way, yes, you did."

"You probably know more about a lot of stuff than most people."

Leaning forward on his elbows, Judd looked her in the eye for a long moment, giving her a rush that flustered her. "From what I've heard about you, Shannon, you're a pretty smart woman yourself."

"What have you heard?"

"Oh, things like you graduated at the top of your class. And you were considering going to medical school after you graduated from high school, but some modeling agency snatched you up and made you sign a contract."

"That's not exactly how it happened, but close enough," she said.

"Wanna tell me the details?"

Shannon narrowed her eyes. "Why would you care?"

"That's a good question. I don't know why I care, but I do."

"Let's see," Shannon said. "I wasn't at the very top of my class. I was second."

"Big whoop."

Shannon chuckled. "I had one fleeting conversation with Janie about majoring in premed in college, but I wasn't serious about it." She paused and sniffled. "Janie's the only person I had this talk with, so now I know who's got a big mouth."

"Cut her some slack, McNab. I called her and pounded the answers out of her. She didn't want to talk, but I threatened bamboo torture."

Once again, Judd made her laugh. "Janie's tough. She's not afraid of anything. She must have wanted you to know, or she wouldn't have told you. I'll have to have a talk with her. I don't want her blabbing my personal life all over town."

"Janie's concerned about you. She's not blabbing anything."

"I know it," Shannon admitted. "But she does need to be careful."

"Does it bother you for me to know things about you?" he asked as he studied her face, making her squirm.

"Well, sort of," she admitted. "I'm not used to letting people see into my life—at least not people I don't know very well."

"I can certainly understand that. I'm kind of the same way."

"You are?" Shannon hadn't seen Judd Manning as a particularly guarded person, so the thought intrigued her.

"Yes, my father was a career military man. He moved the family at the whim of a government that didn't care much about my social life."

"That must have been difficult," Shannon conceded. "Is your father in Atlanta?"

"No, he and my mom live in Arizona, where they retired. I moved here because I always enjoyed staying with my uncle and aunt."

"I've heard some good things about them from Janie," Shannon said. "Janie also told me you're teaching at a Christian school."

"Your friend Janie *is* a big mouth," Judd said.

Shannon laughed as she saw Judd crack a smile. The waitress arrived with two plates stacked with half a dozen pancakes each.

"Whoa!" Shannon said. "I've never eaten that many pancakes at one sitting in my life."

"You haven't lived." He turned to the waitress. "Do you have any of that fabulous blueberry syrup?"

"Coming right up," the waitress said.

"Well?" Judd asked as Shannon chewed her first bite of buttermilk pancakes laden with blueberry syrup. "Like it?"

"Mmm." She stabbed another bite of pancake, stuck it in her mouth, and chewed very slowly. "This is the best thing I've ever tasted."

"Told you."

"We can't come back here, or I'll have to get a whole new wardrobe."

Judd's eyes lit up as he grinned. "Okay, we'll go somewhere else."

❧

Her simple statement gave him hope. She'd said, "We can't come back here," as if she might be considering spending more time with him. If she'd told him, "*I* can't come back here," or "*I* don't want to go out with you," he wouldn't have the hope that had quickened his heart. She'd said, "We—"

"Why are you looking at me like that?" She put her fork down and studied him.

"Oh, nothing. How do you like fondue?"

"Love it."

"Wanna try a new fondue place that just opened on Peachtree Street?"

"Are you trying to make me fat?"

He shrugged. "Quite honestly, I don't really care. You'll still be beautiful."

Her expression suddenly became guarded again as she raised her hand to her cheek. He wanted to kick himself for reminding her of her accident.

"I am so sorry, Shannon," he said softly as he slapped his forehead with the palm of his hand. "I've been such an idiot."

"What?" She regarded him with a curious expression, like she thought he was nuts.

He shook his head and looked at her, then took a sip of his coffee so he could gather his thoughts before saying something stupid again. When he finally did speak, he hoped she'd listen and not shut him out.

"I keep opening my mouth and saying all the wrong things."

"What are you talking about, Judd? Make sense, okay?"

"Let me start over." He paused, borrowing time to run several thoughts through his mind. "Just hear me out, okay?"

Judd started to explain how he'd spent most of his free time taking education classes while working on his master's degree. He told her he'd dated a little, but it wasn't easy for a middle-school English teacher to meet women, and he didn't want to hang out in nightclubs.

"I don't like that either." She gave a quick shudder. "That environment is creepy."

"My sentiments exactly," he agreed and paused to give her a chance to process her thoughts before slamming her with a little-known tidbit about himself. "What I'm trying to tell you, Shannon, is that I don't have much experience with women in a one-on-one relationship."

"Have you ever had a girlfriend?" she asked.

He shrugged. "Once, in eighth grade. But she jilted me when she found out Billy Bateman liked her. I haven't been the same since."

To his delight, Shannon tilted her head back and belted out a laugh. "Poor Judd. But I'm surprised."

"Surprised?" he asked.

"You're a very sweet guy," she began. "And nice-looking and fun to be with, and—"

"Whoa!" He held his hands up. "You're starting to embarrass me. I can't handle all this flattery at once."

"Well, it's the truth."

"Of course it is, but let's not tell all of our secrets, okay? I don't want my head to swell so big that I can't get through the door."

Shannon nodded. He loved her smile, which had returned, and he wasn't about to take any chances with another of his stupid comments.

"I need to run a few errands this morning. We've made quite a dent in the lesson. Maybe we can do this again sometime."

"Yes, I'd like that," she said.

As hard as it was to take her back to her apartment, Judd managed to be stronger than his desire to spend the entire morning with Shannon. He was truthful about the errands. Uncle Garrett had asked him to take the choir robes to the cleaners, and then he needed to go to the school and meet with the parents of one of his students from last year. Shannon could have gone along with him, but too much of a good thing might wind up making her sick of him. He needed to take this nice and slow.

❧

Shannon jumped every time the phone rang, hoping it would be Judd. The afternoon after they'd had breakfast together, she'd opened her apartment door and practically tripped over the Bible study workbook he'd left on the stoop, with a brief note attached that it was hers to keep.

Maybe if she spent a little time working on the lesson on her own, time would pass more quickly. But it didn't. In fact, it dragged even slower than before.

The days literally crawled by. Janie was working late all week, so she couldn't call her. Mom made too much of a fuss over the accident and her scar, so she wasn't in the mood to go to her parents' house.

Why wasn't Judd calling?

Shannon tried to reason with herself, thinking he didn't owe her anything. They'd finished the lesson, so there really wasn't any reason for him to call other than to chat.

Being honest with herself, Shannon knew what she really wanted was to see Judd again. He was fun, interesting, and intelligent, which made her forget her problems.

Maybe seeing the scar bothered him more than he let on, she thought as she studied her reflection in the mirror. Without makeup on, it was still dark pink with tiny dots on each side of the line from the stitches. With makeup, the line was still evident, but it wasn't so bright. Since it itched like crazy from healing, she didn't wear makeup around the apartment. The numbing ointment the doctor had given her was the only thing that soothed the itch. Cold compresses worked in the beginning when there was swelling, but now that seemed pointless.

Finally, after four days had passed, Janie called. "Wanna go to the Bible study Monday night?"

"Of course I want to go," Shannon blurted.

"I don't want to put pressure on you, because I know how you hate that."

"I said I want to go," Shannon repeated.

"It's just that—" Janie stopped before she squealed. "You what? Did I hear you say you wanted to go? This is so great, Shannon. Totally cool."

"I enjoyed it."

"Oh, good." Then Janie grew quiet before adding, "Uh, we need to get you caught up on the lesson. I wouldn't want you to feel lost just because you haven't had a chance to prepare. Maybe Pastor Manning has some extra workbooks. I'll call him right now and ask."

Shannon laughed. "That's all taken care of, Janie. I have the workbook, and I'm up-to-date on the lesson."

"You are?"

"It's about time you stopped yammering and listened." Shannon chuckled. "Judd dropped off a workbook last Tuesday afternoon. And since I'm still not going out much, I've had nothing but time to catch up."

"You have?"

This was the first time Shannon had ever heard her friend at a loss for words. "Yes, I have. I'll be able to sound halfway intelligent in the discussion Monday night."

"How about church tomorrow morning?" Janie asked. "Or is that pushing it?"

"No, I'm fine with church," Shannon replied. "Maybe I can wear a big, floppy hat so people won't be able to see my face."

"Oh, no one wears hats to church anymore."

"I was just kidding, Janie. Lighten up, okay?"

"Uh, okay, that's fine." Silence fell between them for a few seconds before Janie asked, "Since church starts at ten, want me to pick you up at nine thirty?"

"Fine."

"Okay, see you then."

"Janie, you haven't told me what to wear."

"I didn't think you'd need to be told."

Shannon was embarrassed to admit she hadn't been to church in a very long time—not since she'd gone with her parents several years ago. But now she had to.

"It's been a long time, Janie."

Again, silence.

"Janie?"

"Why don't you just wear slacks and a nice top? We're pretty casual, since we're so small and most of the people are pretty young."

After she hung up, Shannon sank further down in the overstuffed chair, allowing the upholstery to envelop her. She was now reaching far out of her comfort zone, with all this church and Bible study business. But it felt right.

Shannon still hadn't heard from Judd since they'd gotten together for breakfast. He had mentioned going out again, so why hadn't she heard from him?

As much as Shannon hated to admit it, she was terribly attracted to Judd, in an odd sort of way. Although he was pleasant to look at, there were plenty of guys around who were better-looking. What she was experiencing went way beyond the physical; it was more of a spiritual and emotional connection.

Judd had admitted to not being a whiz at the Bible, but he was eager to learn more, just as she was, which also surprised her. For the first time in Shannon's life, she was actually thinking about eternal life and what would happen to her soul when her earthly body wore out.

Perhaps the accident had changed her, or maybe she was going through a phase. At any rate, she found herself thinking quite a bit more than usual. For the past eight years, she had been too busy to stop long enough to worry about anything beyond her next photo shoot or Armand's whims.

Shannon picked out something to wear to church and then took a long, relaxing, lavender-scented bubble bath to relax. She needed to get some sleep, or she'd have dark circles to go with her scar.

Her normal nightly routine of flipping through the latest beauty magazines didn't hold her interest, so she picked up her Bible study workbook and began reading ahead. She felt the Holy Spirit working in her heart after she finished the next chapter, and her eyelids fell shut. She awoke as the sun rose, and she felt more rested than she had in a very long time. A smile crept over her face as she remembered she'd see Judd in a few hours.

Janie picked her up at precisely nine thirty. "Anything I need to know before we get there?" Shannon asked as soon as she was safely buckled in her friend's car.

With a shrug, Janie replied, "Only that Judd won't be there this morning. He took some boys on a weekend camping trip, and he won't be back until late tonight."

Disappointment fell over Shannon, but she tried to hide her thoughts and feelings. "That's not what I mean. Is there anything different about church that I need to prepare myself for?"

With a chuckle, Janie shook her head. "No, God's pretty much the same as He was last time you were in church. We have a few songs that are different, and it's a lot more casual, but the message hasn't changed at all."

Shannon finally got to meet Pastor Garrett Manning, a tall, middle-aged man with graying temples and a quick smile. His wife, LaRita, radiated a glow of warmth that drew people close to her. She spoke softly and with sincerity.

"It's so nice to meet you, Shannon," LaRita said as they

shook hands. "Janie has said so many nice things about you."

Pastor Manning came up from behind her. "Judd told us you're thinking about staying in Atlanta."

Shannon shrugged. "I'm not sure yet. It all depends. . ."

Her voice trailed off as she saw his gaze drop down and focus on her scar. Automatically, she reached up to touch it.

"Sorry to hear about the accident," Pastor Manning said. "But you were very fortunate, according to what I hear."

"Yes, I suppose I was." What was with these people, noticing her scar and telling her how fortunate she was?

Janie took Shannon by the arm and tugged. "We need to go find a seat now. See ya later, Pastor. LaRita."

Once they'd gotten away from the pastor and his wife, Janie leaned over and whispered, "You looked like a deer caught in headlights. I had to get you away from there." She patted Shannon on the hand and smiled. "Take a couple deep breaths, sweetie. I don't want to have to scrape you off the floor."

The sermon dealt with compassion and reaching out to those who were less fortunate. Rather than talking about pitying the poor, Pastor Manning spoke of believers sharing their faith with the lost. His words gave Shannon plenty to think about later. She took notes in the margins of her church bulletin.

After the services, Shannon turned down an invitation to join Janie and some of the other singles who had plans to get together at a buffet restaurant. She wanted to get home so she could look up a few things in her Bible. Although it didn't appear she'd have a modeling career anymore, so many years of watching every bite that went into her mouth had become habit and instilled guilt. That would take some time to change, if she ever did.

"I hope you don't mind taking me home first," Shannon said.

Janie shook her head. "Of course I don't mind."

❧

"Did she ask about me?" Judd said when he called Janie right after he got home from the camping trip.

Janie laughed. "She didn't have to. I told her where you were before we got to the church."

"Did she sound disappointed?"

"Look, Judd, you're a grown man. Why don't you call her and find out for yourself?"

"I wanted to give her space."

"Okay, so give her space. You'll see her tomorrow night at the Bible study."

"Yeah," he agreed, "you're right. It's just that. . ."

"You really like her, don't you?"

"Yes, I do."

"Good. I think she likes you, too. But go slowly. Shannon had a double whammy, between the scar and Armand dumping her."

"I remember you telling me about that guy. What a jerk."

"He's not really a jerk," Janie argued. "Armand is actually a very nice man. He's just a little shallow and can't see beyond the scars."

"Janie, you and I both know we all have scars. I'm sure this Armand guy has plenty of his own."

"Yeah, but he does a great job of covering them."

"And Shannon can't see that?" Judd asked.

"I think she does now. You still need to give her time."

"I have all the time in the world."

After they got off the phone, Judd thought about Shannon and how difficult it must have been to have someone she loved turn his back and run when she needed him most. That had to be the most painful part of the whole ordeal.

Judd had been accused of not allowing himself to get close

to women, but he couldn't help himself. Moving so often while growing up had done something to him. Getting close to people was scary, he admitted only to himself. However, he felt different around Shannon. She needed him more than he needed her, and he liked the feeling.

The only thing he wondered was how he'd handle a relationship if the opportunity ever did arise for him to get close to her. It wouldn't be easy for either of them, considering their pasts.

He went over the lesson in the workbook and reread the Bible verses they were supposed to study. For the first time since he'd joined the group, he was prepared to participate without having to resort to clown tactics.

He held back the urge to call Shannon and offer her a ride to the Bible study. He knew it would be best if she went with Janie. He sensed that crowding her would cause her to turn and run from him, and that was the last thing he wanted now.

Paul was the only one at the church when Judd arrived half an hour early. "I see you're eager this evening," Paul chided. "Anything I need to know?"

"Not really," Judd replied with as much nonchalance as he could muster.

With a look of understanding, Paul motioned for Judd to assist with arranging the chairs. "Janie's bringing the food. Why don't you get the coffee started?"

Paul had just left the room, and Judd was about to flip the switch on the coffeepot, when he heard the door open behind him. His hand stilled. He glanced over his shoulder in time to see Shannon and Janie enter the room.

As soon as she spotted him, her lips widened into a glimmering smile, making his heart thud with the anticipation of being near her for a couple of hours. He grinned back, feeling like a foolish adolescent.

"That coffee won't make itself," Janie said as she reached his side. "Ya gotta turn it on."

People began filing into the room, so Judd was forced to broaden his attention. He was still aware of Shannon's presence, something he suspected would always unnerve him.

Once everyone had arrived, they all sat down. Paul started the prayer. Suddenly, the sound of a car backfiring, then squealing tires on the pavement right outside the church filled the room. Judd turned to Shannon to make a wisecrack, but he stopped cold. Shannon's face turned white. Her eyes widened as she jumped up and ran from the room. Judd stood to follow her, but Janie motioned for him to sit back down. "Don't. I'll handle this."

The room grew very quiet as Janie jumped up and flew down the hall after Shannon. Judd's throat constricted as he did what Janie ordered. His ears rang with the hush that fell over the group.

four

Shannon fell against the wall and squeezed her eyes shut. Her heart continued to hammer.

When would the fears go away? Or would they ever?

"Shannon?"

She blinked as she looked up and spotted Janie tentatively approaching, appearing almost afraid to get too close.

"Are you okay?"

Shannon opened her mouth, but no words came out.

"Of course you're not okay. What was I thinking? Want me to take you home?"

Janie continued to step closer, her arms extended, and when she got within reach, she gently placed her arm around Shannon's shoulder.

"You're shaking. Why don't we get you to a place where you can sit down, and I'll pull the car to the door?"

Still numb with fear and shock, Shannon allowed herself to be led to a chair at the end of the long hallway. She sat erect, her hands folded in her lap, staring straight ahead. When Janie came back, she didn't move.

Although she could see, she was numb. Her ears rang, and her mouth was dry.

"Shannon." Janie tugged on her hand, but Shannon couldn't move. Her legs felt like they were filled with lead. "Your hand's icy cold. Let me see if someone can help us, okay? Wait here."

The car's backfire had long since passed, but the memory of the sharp sound echoed in Shannon's head. The only thing she felt was a numbing fear as it held her in its clutches.

❧

Judd held his breath as he paced and waited to hear how Shannon was. When Janie appeared at the door, he shot over toward her.

Crooking a finger, Janie motioned for Gretta, a woman Judd knew was a nurse in the local hospital emergency room. "I think she's in shock. Can you come take a look at her?"

Now there was nothing that could hold Judd back. He might not know much about medicine, but he did know how he felt about Shannon.

When Janie looked at him, he tightened his jaw. She wouldn't dare tell him he couldn't go to Shannon. Janie didn't say a word when he followed her and Gretta to where Shannon sat staring blankly ahead.

Judd stood back a few feet while Gretta checked Shannon's vital signs. He closed his eyes and said a brief prayer for healing for her and guidance for himself. Shannon's car crash had caused more trauma that he'd realized—and much more devastation than a scar on the face.

"How's she doing?" Paul asked from behind. He kept his voice low, almost to a whisper.

Judd quickly turned around and took a step back so Shannon wouldn't overhear. "I'm not sure yet. She looks pretty shaken."

"I can imagine. What she went through was serious."

"Yeah, I know."

Janie took a step back and joined them. "I've never seen her like this, and I've known her since we were little."

"Any idea what we can do?" Paul asked.

"Just be there for her. Let her know you care."

"I do care," Judd said.

Janie looked at him for a moment before turning back to her friend.

"Why don't you stay close by and be there when she comes out of this trance?" Janie's expression was one of concern and deep affection. Judd could tell hers and Shannon's friendship was strong.

"I'll do whatever it takes," he replied.

He didn't want to interfere. However, when Gretta turned and said she thought Shannon would be fine in a few minutes, he didn't waste a single second. He was beside Shannon before anyone could stop him.

He took her hand in his and felt the clamminess. At least she didn't pull away.

"Want me to take you home?" he asked.

Shannon blinked at him before slowly turning toward Janie, who tilted her head and held her hands out to her side.

"Your decision, Shannon," she said. "I just want you to be comfortable."

All eyes turned back to Shannon to see what she'd say. She finally nodded. She tried to stand on her own, but her wobbly legs gave out, and she fell back onto the chair.

"Put your arm around my neck, and I'll walk you to my car," Judd said softly, hoping to offer comfort to this broken woman. He stuck his hand in his pocket and pulled out a set of keys. "Janie, would you mind running out to my car and pulling it closer to the exit?"

"Sure thing."

Janie grabbed the keys and took off running. Judd positioned Shannon to make it easier for her to walk.

He loved the way her body felt next to his. Although she was still shaky, she was firm and athletic—nothing like a frail woman who nibbled rabbit food to keep her weight down.

As they hobbled down the hallway toward the exit, he inhaled the spicy fragrance from her hair whenever it brushed across his face. He wanted to lean over and bury his face in her hair, but he wouldn't dare do anything so bold and presumptuous.

Once they got to the door, she stopped and shifted, pulling away a little. He hated that he had to let go of her in order to get the door.

Janie pulled up at the exact moment that they reached the edge of the sidewalk. "You sure you wanna do this?" Janie asked.

"Positive. Go on back inside and finish the Bible study. I'll take her back to her place and make sure she's okay before I leave."

"Thanks, Judd." Janie smiled at him in appreciation. "You're a good guy. No, make that a *great* guy." She leaned over and snapped Shannon's seat belt into place, then slammed the car door shut.

Judd cringed at the harsh sound, until he glanced over and saw that it hadn't fazed Shannon.

Once Judd was buckled in, he turned back to Shannon. He was surprised to see her staring at him, a half-smile on her lips.

"Feeling better?" he asked.

She nodded. "A little."

He offered a few minutes of silence to let her recover and regroup. Her ordeal had taken its toll on her in a big way. Although he knew he couldn't be beside her every minute of every day, he wanted to help her as much as possible right now.

"Wanna hear some music?" he asked. Maybe that would drown out outside noises and help her relax.

"Sure. That's fine."

Judd turned on the radio and pushed the button he had tuned to the contemporary Christian music station. The sounds of a heavy metal band blasted through the car.

Shannon flinched. He quickly hit the POWER button and silenced it.

"Sorry."

She managed a weak smile. "You didn't know. What kind of music is that?"

"Christian rock, believe it or not."

"Amazing."

When Judd pulled up to a stop sign, he took the opportunity to study her in the light of the streetlamp. Good. Her hands weren't shaking anymore, and her eyes didn't have that glazed look.

When they reached her apartment complex, he pulled into a parking spot and instructed her to stay put so he could walk her to her door. This time she was much steadier on her feet, but he didn't let go, just in case.

She had the presence of mind to dig in her purse and have her key ready before getting out of the car. He stood, feeling rather awkward, while she unlocked her door. What should he do now? Leave her alone and risk something happening to her, or ask if he could come in?

Holding the door open, Shannon turned around and touched him on the arm.

"Would you like to come inside?"

"I, uh. . ."

"Please?" Her one simple plea turned him inside-out. "Are you sure?"

"I insist. Come on in, and I'll fix you a cup of chamomile tea."

"Okay, I'll come in, but let me fix the tea. You lie down on the couch."

Shannon snickered. "Such a caregiver. Not many guys are like that."

"Well, I am a teacher, and I'm used to watching after children."

The instant he said that, he knew it was a mistake. Her eyebrows shot up.

"I'm not a child," she said firmly.

"No," he said, trying to think of the best way to backpedal. "I didn't mean it like it sounded. What I meant was. . ."

"No, don't explain. I understand."

"You do?"

"Yes. I'm always sticking my foot in my mouth, so I know how things can come out completely wrong."

Judd couldn't believe she was being so nice about his stupid comment. "At the risk of sounding insensitive, let me get the tea started."

Shannon tilted her head back and belted out a hearty laugh. He felt a joyous sensation coursing through him at the sound of her happiness. She was doing much better than she had been back at the church.

"That's not insensitive at all," she said. "In fact, I find you to be a very sensitive man."

"Sensitive, but strong," he said, playfully flexing a muscle.

"Oh, yes, of course. Very strong. Macho, in fact."

"Let's not get too carried away. We don't want this to go to my head."

Judd left Shannon sitting on the couch with the remote pointed at the TV. As he rummaged through the cupboards, he once again found himself in prayer—something that was happening more often these days.

Lord, I pray for wisdom as Shannon and I get to know each other. Guide us in our relationship and help us get closer to You.

"The tea bags are on the little shelf to the left of the stove," Shannon called out. "Use the big mugs on the mug tree."

"Sure thing."

Judd made himself at home in Shannon's kitchen. He was fascinated and amused by the way everything matched with a pig motif—from the small row of tea tins on the shelf beside the stove, to the mugs and wire rack they hung from.

Once the tea had finished steeping, Judd carried both mugs into the living room, where Shannon sat with her legs curled beneath her. She accepted her tea with a smile as she patted the cushion next to her.

"I'll sit over here." He chose the chair that was angled toward her position on the couch. "I can see you better."

He wasn't about to sit next to her now. Every time he caught a whiff of her fresh, clean scent, he felt an overwhelming urge to wrap his arms around her and draw her closer.

"Mm, this is good," she said as she sipped the tea.

"There really wasn't much to it. Just heat the water and pour over the tea bag."

"Some men can't even do that."

Judd opened his mouth to make one of his typical sarcastic comments about men who couldn't boil water, but he caught himself. That might touch on something that would send her over the edge again.

"Can you cook?" she asked with interest.

"Oh, yeah," he replied. "I heat up a mean can of soup."

Her smile brought a flash of sunshine into the room. "How about real food?"

"A few things. Roast beef, baked chicken, meatloaf, chili, spaghetti. Usual stuff."

"I'm impressed."

"How about you?" he asked. "How are your culinary skills?"

"Not good, I'm afraid. My mom always shooed me out of the kitchen. She told me I didn't need to cook with my looks."

Surprisingly, she didn't sound conceited when she said that. Her statement was very matter-of-fact rather than boastful.

"So you've always wanted to be a model?"

"My mom wanted that. I wasn't sure what I wanted, so I figured I might as well go after her dream."

Her confession hit him hard. How many times had he

heard about the expectations of parents forcing their children to do what they had no business doing? More than he could count, that's for sure.

"Did you like modeling?"

"Some of it, but not all. A lot of people think it's all glamour and fun."

"That's what I would've thought." Judd blew into his tea before taking another sip. "Is it really bad?"

"No, not bad. Just constraining. I had to watch everything I put in my mouth. I couldn't get sunburned when I went to the beach. Even tan lines could be a problem if I had to model clothes."

"Yeah, I can see where tan lines might be bad."

She took a sip of tea before adding, "Not to mention the big blemish that would pop up the day before a big shoot. It never failed."

"Oh, that had to be awful. I feel sorry for the makeup artist having to deal with that one."

Shannon's warm smile let him know his teasing wasn't painful for her. That was a huge relief. "How about you? Have you always wanted to be a teacher?"

"No, not really. I never knew what I wanted, but I figured I like kids, and English is something I understand. It seemed like the most natural thing to get into."

A flash of pain shot through her expression. She glanced down into her mug as if all her thoughts centered in the hot, steamy liquid.

"I'm sorry."

Her head quickly shot up, and she looked at him quizzically. "Sorry? For what?"

"For upsetting you."

"You didn't upset me. You just made me think."

"I hate making people think. Forgive me."

"There you go again." Her laughter was rich and genuine. "I like being around you, Judd. You're such a happy person."

"I like being around you, too, Shannon," he said as he stood. "But unfortunately, I need to leave. Tomorrow morning comes awfully early, and I have to get up with the birds."

Shannon walked him to the door. He saw that she was steady on her feet. "Thanks, Judd. I don't know what I'd do without you."

He suddenly felt awkward, like one of the seventh grade boys in his classes. Should he just tell her good-bye and leave? Or should he risk a kiss?

Taking a chance and pulling up all the courage he could, he leaned toward her and dropped a quick kiss on her lips before backing away. She grinned and waved.

❧

Shannon never imagined herself in this situation, with such an intense feeling for anyone besides Armand. Judd's simple, chaste kiss had sent tingles down her spine and made her feel all wobble-kneed.

As soon as she closed the door behind him, she headed for her bedroom. It wasn't very late, but the ordeal of going into shock over some stupid car backfiring had wiped her out.

She changed into her nightgown and crawled under the covers, hoping to get plenty of rest so she could think straight in the morning. However, thoughts of Judd kept popping into her mind, preventing her from falling asleep. Her lips still tingled from the sweetest kiss she'd ever had.

She eventually gave up and flipped on the light beside her bed. Maybe reading something would make her sleepy.

At first, she reached for a fashion magazine, but it bored her to tears. She got up and wandered around the apartment, until she spotted her Bible on the kitchen table. *Maybe this'll help*, she thought.

Curling up with the Bible and a concordance she'd gotten from Janie, Shannon figured she needed to see what God had to say about her fears.

Her concordance showed a long list of scriptures that spoke of fear, so Shannon looked up each one and tried to relate to what it said. Finally, she read Matthew chapter fourteen, verses twenty-two through thirty-six and found comfort. Surely, if Jesus could protect Peter on the stormy sea, He'd watch over her in this turbulent time.

Although she'd never immersed herself in the Word before, Shannon never questioned the existence of Jesus—or that He was the Son of God. But until now, she hadn't given Him much thought.

She read the passage over and over, shutting her eyes occasionally to let it sink in. Just as Jesus had reached out His hand to Peter, He had offered a hand to Shannon and allowed her to survive the horrible car crash. There had to be a reason she'd gone through it, just as there was a reason she'd survived. Could it be that He'd allowed her tragedy so she'd slow down and pay attention to Him?

Finally, she closed the Bible and turned off the light. Darkness only seemed to enhance the sounds of night, causing her heart to hammer in her chest.

For several minutes, Shannon stared up at the ceiling, illuminated by the moonlight that filtered through the sheers on her window. Christ's love filled her heart as she accepted Him as her Savior. Eventually, she shut her eyes and prayed.

Lord, Jesus, my life is in Your hands. I know you don't want me to be fearful like this, but I don't know what to do to make the horrors of my experience go away. Please show me what you want me to do.

She let out a deep sigh before finally whispering, "Amen."

❧

The sound of the telephone startled Shannon from her sound

sleep. She lifted her head and glanced at the clock on the nightstand as she reached for the receiver. It was already after eight.

"Don't tell me you're still sleeping," Janie said.

"Afraid so," Shannon replied as she sat up and rubbed her sleepy eyes.

"You okay?"

"I guess. I had a hard time going to sleep last night."

"Judd was really worried about you. I hope you didn't mind me letting him take you home."

"Of course I didn't mind. He's very sweet."

"Do you need anything?"

"Like what?"

"I don't know," Janie said. "Like maybe someone to come over for a little while? I can take off work if you need me."

Shannon managed a chuckle. "I'm not that bad off—not yet, anyway. Don't take time off work for me."

"I'll do it, you know."

"Yes, I know you will. And I really appreciate that."

"You have my work number, right?"

"Yes," Shannon replied, "and your cell phone number."

"Don't hesitate to call me if you need me."

"Okay, okay."

"Promise?"

"Stop trying to mother me, Janie. I'm a big girl. I can be alone."

"Yeah, but—"

"Don't worry so much. I just had a little setback last night. I'll be just fine."

"Well, if you're sure. . ."

"I'm positive. Now go on and get to work. I need to get up and do a few things around here."

After they hung up, Shannon stepped into her slippers,

grabbed her Bible, and trudged through her apartment. She started the coffee before sitting down to go over the Bible verses she'd read the night before. It was amazing how much peace she got from reading scripture and realizing how much Peter had to rely on God. Jesus never let him down, just as He promised He'd never let her down.

Later in the afternoon, after Shannon finished straightening the apartment, her mother dropped by.

"Have you even left the apartment at all today?" her mom asked.

"No, not yet."

"You really shouldn't be sitting around this place, Shannon. You need to get out, be around people."

Her mom had stormed through the living room to the kitchen. She put several plastic containers into the refrigerator before plunking her purse on the dining room table and rummaging through it. She whipped out a couple of brochures featuring young, perfect-looking women on the front.

"I've gotten some information about plastic surgery. I thought you might want to start looking around for someone to take care of your. . .scar."

Shannon reached up and touched her cheek. Her mother made the same face she always did and quickly looked away.

"You don't have to live with that, you know."

"I know, but I'm not ready to have plastic surgery."

"You don't want to wait too long, Shannon."

"It hasn't been that long. Let me rest for a little while and figure out what I need to do."

Her mother turned to face her, planted her fist on her hip, and shook her head. "Shannon McNab, you're smarter than you're acting. You know as well as I do that your agent won't be able to hold everyone off much longer. All your accounts will start looking for a replacement if you don't come back soon. You need to get better as quickly as possible, or your career might be over."

"Would that be so bad?" Shannon asked defiantly.

"How can you say something like that?" her mother shrieked. "You know that would be awful. You've worked too long and hard to let it come to this. You're a supermodel. That's what you do. That's who you are."

Shannon fought the urge to argue with her mother. Being a supermodel was only what she did for a living—not who she was. But arguing with Sara McNab was futile—this was something she knew from experience. Once that woman set her mind to something, she was a shark. She chomped down and never let go. Shannon pursed her lips and offered a slight nod, holding back all her thoughts and frustrations.

Her mother reached out and gently touched her undamaged cheek. "I'll leave the list of plastic surgeons for you to look at when you're feeling a little better. Don't wait too long."

"Thanks, Mom," Shannon said.

"I can tell you're still pretty down about this, Shannon. The only thing that'll snap you out of this mood is getting back to work. Trust me."

Taking the path of least resistance, Shannon let her mother talk. There was nothing she could say to change her mind. All her mom had ever wanted for Shannon was fame and fortune—mostly because that had been what she'd wanted in her own life many years ago. Instead, she'd gotten married and had Shannon six months later, which had killed her dreams of acting or modeling. Besides, enough people had told Sara that she was too short to be taken seriously as a model, and her Southern accent was too thick to make it as an actress—which was why she'd enrolled Shannon in diction classes at a very young age.

"I don't want my daughter sounding like a bumpkin," she'd

told everyone who stood still long enough to listen.

As Shannon's mother chattered incessantly about all the things they'd do to get her back on her modeling career path, Shannon pretended to listen. Instead, she kept thinking about the scripture she'd read to find comfort.

When silence fell between them, Shannon turned to her mom. "We used to go to church when I was little. But I was wondering. . .well. . .have you ever read the Bible, Mom?"

"Some of it. Back when I was a little girl, my parents made me go to Sunday school. They made me memorize Bible verses." Tilting her head to one side, she offered a questioning look. "Why?"

Shannon shrugged. "I was just wondering if you ever stopped to think about all the things Jesus did for us."

Looking a little stunned, her mother let out a nervous giggle. "All that Bible stuff took place a long time ago, Shannon. This is now. I'm sure God would want you to go back to your job and not worry about such things."

"I'm not worried," Shannon said.

"Look, sweetheart, I really need to run. Some of the women at the club are expecting me. Let me know if you need something, okay?"

"Sure, Mom."

After a quick air kiss, Shannon showed her mother to the door. After closing it, she let out a breath of frustration. Obviously, her mom hadn't given much thought to her faith. Just as obviously, talking about it made her very uncomfortable. Shannon understood. She'd been the same way until her first brush with Janie's Bible study group.

Shannon went back to her room to play with her makeup when the doorbell rang again. Probably her mother. She must have forgotten something.

She went to the door and yanked it open. There stood

Judd, grinning, a cake server in one hand and a plastic sack dangling from the other.

"Hi, there. Thought you might be hungry."

"Not really," Shannon admitted. "My mom brought some food, but I haven't gotten into it yet."

"I'm sure it's better than what I have, but remember, it's the thought that counts." He nodded toward the kitchen, and Shannon moved out of his way. "Maybe you can eat just a little for me."

Judd's very presence brought a smile to Shannon's face. She followed him and watched as he put a big round plastic cake server on the counter. Then he stuck a couple tubs of yogurt on the top shelf of her refrigerator. He groped around the bottom of the bag and pulled out some Ramen noodles that he placed on the counter beside the cake server.

Shannon pointed to the plastic container. "What's that?"

"German chocolate cake. I hope you like it."

It had been years since she'd tasted German chocolate cake, but she remembered how it tasted.

"I love it," she said as her mouth watered. "How about the noodles? What kind?"

"I wasn't sure what flavor you liked," he said, "so I just grabbed some creamy chicken."

"Mm, my favorite."

"Want me to fix it for you?"

"No, you took care of me last night. Now it's my turn to take care of you."

"I really don't mind."

Shannon stabbed her finger toward the kitchen table. "Sit."

five

"Yes, ma'am."

Not wasting a second, Judd did as he was told.

Shannon leaned over and checked out the contents of the refrigerator. She pulled out one of the bowls her mom had brought and placed it on the counter.

"I'm not the best cook in the world, but I can heat stuff up."

"That's all that matters," Judd said as he watched her with interest.

It took Shannon less than five minutes to microwave the vegetables and turkey her mother had brought, as well as cooking the noodles from Judd. She piled two plates and bowls with food, a heaping one for him and one with much smaller servings for herself.

He frowned at her plate before offering her a questioning glance.

"I'm really not that hungry," she reminded him.

"This food wasn't for me. I brought it for you to get your strength back."

"I know, but I hate eating alone."

"In that case, let's chow down. But first, I want to say a blessing."

Shannon bowed her head as he said a short prayer of thanksgiving for the food on the table. When he said, "Amen," she opened one eye and caught him staring at her, smiling.

"What?" she asked. "Were you peeking?"

"No, of course not."

"Then why are you looking at me like that?"

"I'm happy to be here," he replied. "Let's eat."

Judd scarfed his food down quickly, while Shannon nibbled at hers. She was sure he noticed she hadn't eaten much, but he didn't say anything.

With each bite she took, he seemed to relax a little. He even made a few comments, like "Atta girl" and "That'll make you feel much better."

It made her uncomfortable that he was watching, even though she liked having him there. She knew she needed to eat, but she didn't need an audience cheering her on.

Finally, she put down her fork and pushed her chair back. "I can't eat any more."

He slowly nodded. "I understand. I guess I'd better get going. I have papers to grade and stuff to do tonight. Let me know if you need anything, okay?"

"Of course."

"Oh, one more thing," he said as he reached the door. "I'd like to get together with you one more time before the next Bible study." He tilted his head forward and looked at her from beneath his heavy eyebrows. "That is, if you plan to go back to the church."

"Of course I do."

"Good."

Shannon bit her bottom lip.

"How about tomorrow night?" he said.

Maybe if she agreed, she'd have a little peace. Although it was nice having him here for a little while, being under such intense scrutiny wore her out. "Okay, tomorrow night's fine."

"Seven okay?"

"Sure, seven's fine."

For a second, it looked like Judd might kiss her again. She braced herself for the sensation, wanting it but dreading it at the same time. When he backed away instead, she felt awkward, almost like a teenage girl who didn't have a clue what to do around a guy.

She hated her vulnerable state. Her mental health and emotional state were even harder to deal with than her scar. There was no doubt in her mind that the giddiness over being around Judd was mostly the result of feeling alone and without the safety net of Armand or work.

And there was this Christianity thing. It baffled her. She'd always been happy and carefree before she'd ever gone to a single Bible study. Why did she suddenly feel this huge weight of responsibility to study scripture? Was it part of overcoming her trauma? Or was it something else?

Reading the Bible made sense while she was doing it or when she was with the group from the church talking about their faith. But now, alone and confused, she wondered if it was more of a crutch than anything—something she was using to make herself feel better.

Her mind whirred with all sorts of crazy thoughts, flip-flopping back and forth between the desire to lean on the Lord and wanting to go it alone. As she picked up her Bible and flipped through it, stopping to randomly read scripture, she became more confused than ever and worked her way into a state of exhaustion.

After changing into her gown, she sat on the edge of her bed and contemplated an appropriate prayer. What should she pray for? Healing? Her relationship with Judd? Answers to her questions about the Bible?

Finally, she bowed her head and said a general prayer, touching on everything she'd been thinking. If nothing else, it felt good to get it off her mind.

She woke up the next morning feeling more refreshed than she had since the accident. Her first thought went straight to her bedtime prayer the night before.

Feeling better made it so much easier for Shannon to function throughout the day. She managed to shower, dress, and get through her chores without dreading her next step, as she had so many times since the accident.

Her emotional state had leveled, at least for the time being—until another car backfired. Now was the time for her to prepare herself for her future and any surprises she might encounter along the way. She needed to do something to continue feeling better.

The problem was, she didn't know where to start. Should she make an appointment with a psychologist or psychiatrist? That seemed pretty drastic right now, in the light of day.

Glancing over at the brochures her mother had left on the table, Shannon thought about plastic surgery. Would that help? It certainly couldn't hurt.

She picked up the list of certified plastic surgeons, headed to the phone, and stopped in her tracks. What was she thinking? She hadn't even given the scar time to heal on its own. How would anyone know what needed to be done? Besides, what was the purpose of getting plastic surgery? She wasn't sure she wanted to go back to modeling.

Shannon let out a huge sigh. If she kept thinking like this, she knew she'd make herself crazy. So she grabbed her purse, her car keys, and headed for the door.

She hadn't driven since the crash. The brand-new car her parents had delivered still sat in the parking lot, shiny and waiting.

Sucking in a deep breath, she forged ahead, moving with determination to get over this major hurdle of driving a car for the first time since she'd been hit.

As she slid in behind the wheel, she felt fear clutching at her throat. *Okay, you can do this. Just take it one step at a time.*

She stuck her key in the ignition, took a deep breath, and

started the engine. So far, so good.

Knowing how susceptible she was to a panic attack, she decided to take her first spin around the block before venturing out any further. Heart pounding in her chest, she pulled to the stop sign at the road and waited for all cars to pass before pulling out.

Shannon made her way around the block, not blinking, talking to herself, being extra cautious as cars approached from all sides. She jumped at the sound of a car honking behind her.

One quick glance at the speedometer let her know she was driving way too slow. She offered a wave to the person behind her and accelerated a little harder. But not too fast. Each mile per hour she increased seemed to speed up her heart rate.

Finally, when she took her last turn back into the parking lot, she blew out the breath she'd been holding. She'd done it. She'd gotten back behind the wheel and driven—something she wasn't certain she'd ever be able to do.

It wasn't until she got out of her car and stood up that she realized how traumatic her experience had actually been. Her knees buckled beneath her, and she had to grab on to the car to keep from falling to the asphalt.

Shannon knew she needed help. And she needed it very soon.

She spent the rest of the afternoon contemplating what kind of help she needed to seek. After being away from Atlanta so long, she had no idea who to call. Janie had always been such a together person, so she probably didn't know anyone to refer her to. Her mother's solution to the problem would be to get plastic surgery and head straight back to a modeling career, hopefully picking up where she left off.

Then she thought about Judd. She felt more comfortable around him than anyone besides Janie. Surely, she could talk to him about this, and he'd understand. Maybe he'd know someone, or at least have a direction to point her toward. Now, with that settled, Shannon headed for the kitchen to whip up something healthy for dinner. She needed to get back to as normal a life as possible, and just because she didn't see herself going back to modeling didn't mean she shouldn't be careful what she put into her mouth.

The phone rang exactly half an hour after Judd was scheduled to get out of school. He'd been calling her every day at the same time, asking how she was doing.

"Whatcha been up to all day?" he asked as he always did.

She found comfort in the familiarity of his voice. "You're not going to believe this, but I drove a little."

"You're right! I don't believe it. Where'd you go?"

"Just around the block."

If she'd been talking to anyone else, Shannon wouldn't even have mentioned her short excursion, but she felt completely comfortable with him. He seemed to understand the significance of what she'd done.

"That's a great start. And not a bad idea. You can go just a little farther each day until you're back to your old self."

Good. He'd given her an opening to ask her question.

"Speaking of getting back to my old self, do you know anyone I can talk to?"

"You can talk to me, Shannon."

"I know. But I mean about some deep things. Like mental problems."

"Mental problems?" he asked. "I don't think you have mental problems. What you're dealing with is a normal fear after an immensely traumatic experience."

"Whatever you want to call it, I need to talk to someone."

"How about my uncle?"

"The pastor?"

"Yeah, he's pretty good with things like this."

"I don't know."

"Tell you what, Shannon; let me talk to him and see what he says. He might be able to help you, and if he can't, he can refer you to someone who can."

She paused for a few seconds. "Okay, that's fine."

"Now, for tonight. Since you're driving, would you like to meet somewhere?"

"I haven't worked up the courage to drive at night yet."

"Okay, I'll pick you up. How about dinner? Do you have plans?"

Shannon remembered the extra large salad she'd made and put in the refrigerator. It was plenty big enough for both of them if she added a little of the chicken her mother had brought.

"Why don't you come over here for dinner?"

"I thought you couldn't cook."

"I can't. I just tossed some romaine in a bowl with a few tomatoes and some celery. Mom brought marinated chicken breasts. I thought we could have that."

"Yum. You make healthy eating sound good. What time do you want me there?"

❧

As soon as Shannon gave him the time, they hung up. He then turned around and dialed his uncle's office number at the church.

"Hey, Judd. Whatcha need?"

Judd told him about Shannon's need to seek counseling. "I think she's got a few issues she hasn't told me about, and she needs someone to give her some guidance."

"I'll be glad to talk to her, Judd. What's her number?"

After giving his uncle Shannon's number, Judd hung up and grabbed the shopping list Aunt LaRita had given him.

Although his aunt and uncle had told him he could live with them rent-free until he saved enough for his own place, he insisted on helping out wherever possible. LaRita had reluctantly given in and handed over occasional lists that freed her up to do some of the charity work she enjoyed.

Without another moment of hesitation, he ran the errands, then went home to put things away. A quick shower and shave later, Judd was on his way to Shannon's place.

She greeted him at the door, wearing a pink velour jogging suit and running shoes, with her blond hair hanging naturally over her shoulders. She was beautiful in spite of the scar she hadn't bothered trying to hide with makeup.

"Your uncle called almost right after we hung up. You don't waste time, do you?"

"No, there's no point. What'd he say?"

"I have an appointment with him tomorrow afternoon."

"Talking about not wasting time. Must be genetic."

"I just hope he doesn't think I'm shallow and self-absorbed."

Judd felt a thud in his chest at the look of helplessness on her face. "Why would he think something like that?"

"I don't know." She held her hands up as she shook her head. "It just seems that all I can think about anymore is how I feel about things. *My* fears, *my* career, *my* happiness. Somehow, it all seems so wrong to be thinking about myself so much."

"I think that's all normal stuff to think about."

"Yeah, but not to this degree."

"You've got to give yourself some time, Shannon. You've just been through one of the most harrowing experiences a person can have. Be patient with yourself."

She audibly sighed. He watched the range of emotions flit across her face. She finally nodded.

"You're probably right. But I still need to get help. I can't do this alone."

"You're not alone. You have a whole bunch of people praying for you."

She smiled. "I know, and I appreciate every prayer that's offered."

Something had changed in her. Judd noticed that, even when she gave lip service to accepting prayer, she didn't seem to believe it like she had a couple days ago.

"Come on into the kitchen. The salads are ready. All I have to do is make some tea, and we can eat."

Following her into the kitchen, Judd noticed how her strides were long and purposeful. As each day passed, she was getting stronger physically, but she obviously didn't realize it. He was beginning to see the confidence of a world-class supermodel. That was good, but he worried she'd eventually have no use for someone as normal and plain as him.

Once they were seated at the kitchen table, Shannon propped her elbows on the table and leaned toward him.

"You wanna say the blessing, or do you want me to?"

"It doesn't matter," Judd said. "Whatever you want."

"Hey, what's going on? Are you okay?"

"Sure, I'm fine," he replied with a smile. "Why don't you say the blessing?"

"Thank you, Lord, for the blessing of this food," she began, sounding unsure of herself. "We're thankful for your kindness and mercy. Amen."

As she spoke, Judd wondered where her conviction was. She certainly didn't sound sincere. Something had happened to her since he'd last seen her.

She chatted happily as they ate. He didn't have to say much, which suited him just fine. Once they were finished, he stood to carry the dishes to the sink.

"Leave those," she told him. "Let's get started on the Bible study. I'm eager to get ahead again."

Judd didn't argue with her. He followed her into the living room and sat on the chair across from the loveseat where she'd flopped.

Throughout the evening, he felt somewhat mechanical, just going through the motions of discussion and answering questions. Finally, when they got to the end of the week's lesson, he shut his workbook.

"Well, I guess that's it for now. I need to run. I have to get up early in the morning for school. We're doing poetry this week, and I always start each day reading some of my favorite poems."

"You like poetry?" she said, sounding surprised.

"Of course. I'm an English teacher."

"What's your favorite?"

Judd shrugged. "Anything but the dark stuff. I have to admit, I tend to be a romantic when it comes to poetry."

Suddenly, her eyes glazed over. He must have said something wrong, because the bright, cheery smile she wore had suddenly disappeared.

"Good night, Shannon," Judd said as he walked out the door where she stood, holding it open. "See you soon."

"Yeah," she replied. "G'night."

Whatever had happened in her apartment was a mystery to him. While nothing physical had happened, it seemed like the night had been a major turning point—and not in a good direction. His heart sank at the memory of the look on her face as he left.

❧

Armand had loved poetry, too, Shannon remembered. But he was the opposite of Judd. His favorite poet was Poe, king of darkness.

After Judd left, she closed and locked the door before going to the kitchen to clean up the small mess from dinner. He'd offered to help, and perhaps she should have let him, but she didn't want him to see how much effort she was having to put into maintaining her equilibrium.

He kept looking at her, almost as if he was confused by something. That had made her very uncomfortable and self-conscious.

She noticed that he was quiet tonight, almost moody. He'd tried to pretend nothing was wrong, but she could tell something bothered him.

After the dishes were done, she went through her nightly routine of flipping through magazines, channel surfing, then giving up and going to bed. She grabbed her Bible off the loveseat where she'd left it and placed it on the nightstand. After she got ready for bed, she picked it up, looked at the cover, then put it back. She was tired. She didn't feel like reading or trying to find comfort in scripture at the moment. Her heart felt too heavy for something like a gospel message to be able to help.

After a long night of tossing and turning, Shannon crawled out of bed and plodded to the bathroom. Leaning over the sink, she studied her face in the mirror and took a really good, long look at her scar. It was still bad.

Then she thought about the guy who'd hit her. He was dead. Although people around her had tried to cover the details, she'd learned that he had a wife and young children. Yes, it was his fault that he'd been drinking and should never have been behind the wheel. But what about those kids? They were innocent, and just because of some stupid error in judgment on their father's part, they'd grow up without a father. Shannon couldn't imagine what life would have been like without her dad in her life.

Her parents had been complete opposites. Where her mother was always looking over her shoulder and wishing for things that never could be, her father taught her to count her blessings and enjoy life. Her mother was focused on her own desires; her father was active with Habitat for Humanity. He'd been in construction all his life, so he figured that was the best way he could give back to those less fortunate.

Maybe she could find out something about the family of the man who'd smashed into her. If his family needed something done around their house, perhaps she could talk to her father about helping out. It wasn't much, but at least it would be something. Plus, she had a nice nest egg that would more than provide a decent living for the rest of her life. It wouldn't hurt much to help them out financially.

Shannon kept a close eye on the clock. She didn't want to be late for her appointment with Pastor Manning. Although she seriously doubted he'd be able to help her, hopefully he knew someone she could go to for psychological help. Being in his profession, he must know people in all fields. In fact, she might even try enlisting his help with the family.

Pastor Manning greeted her at his office door, his hand extended, a warm smile on his face. She instantly felt comfortable and able to open up to him without holding back.

"Why don't we sit over here where we can be more comfortable?" he said, gesturing toward a conversational seating arrangement of a worn but matching sofa, loveseat, and chair.

Within minutes, she found herself babbling about every thought she'd had on her mind since the accident and even some things she'd been pondering before her trip home. He continued to nod and make brief comments to encourage her.

Finally, she flopped back on the couch. "I can't believe how much I just talked. I didn't give you a chance to get a word in edgewise." She paused for a second and smiled. "Just call me motormouth. That's what all my friends called me back in high school."

"Motormouth, huh?" He nodded and chuckled. "I guess that's a term of endearment if it comes from the right people."

"Oh, only my closest friends would dare call me that." Then, Shannon started going on and on about Janie and some of her other friends before she realized she was at it again. "Oops! Sorry."

"No, that's quite all right. I like to hear you talk. You're a delightful young woman and a great conversationalist."

She laughed. "I guess that's a nice way of putting it."

Pastor Manning's smile slowly faded as he leaned forward in his chair across from Shannon, clasped his hands, and looked at the floor for a moment before meeting her gaze. "I understand you're having a rough time dealing with some things. Would you like to talk about it?"

She started to tell him she only wanted a referral, but he was so easy to talk to, and he truly did seem to care. After a brief pause, she nodded.

"Yes, I am having a hard time."

"I'm listening."

Shannon started slowly, telling him how consuming being a supermodel was and how she was never allowed to forget about what she did for a living. There was always someone there to remind her, like cameras, crew, fans, and Armand. Although she'd once thought she loved him, she now realized he was the path of least resistance—the way she chose to go to keep up the pretense of living the perfect life.

"Do you still hear from him?" Pastor Manning asked.

"No. He left right after the bandages were removed. Sure, he sent flowers and a couple of postcards, but that's it. My relationship with him is over."

"Are you sure?"

"Positive."

"Does this upset you?"

"No, not really," Shannon replied truthfully. "After being apart from him for this long, I see how it was all just for show, not to mention convenience. We were both in the same profession, and we understood each other. Neither of us ever wondered if the other had ulterior motives."

"Sounds like you might have been mistaken about that."

"Maybe." Shannon grew silent as she thought about his comment. Perhaps she was mistaken, and they did have ulterior motives. Their motives could have been to appease those around them rather than joining together as two people who truly loved each other. That was very possible. Highly likely, in fact.

Pastor Manning studied his steepled fingers before looking back at her. "Sounds like you're also having problems dealing with the fact that the accident involved a death."

"Yes, that's really bugging me," she admitted.

"I can certainly understand that. But you should never feel guilty. It was completely out of your control."

"Yes, I know," she agreed. Then she told him what she'd overheard about the man's family.

"You have a good heart, Shannon. I'm sure the Lord would love for you to give to the man's family. That shows the forgiveness in your heart."

"Oh, it's not out of forgiveness."

"Is it from guilt?"

Slowly, she nodded, admitting her shortcoming. "Afraid so."

"That's something you need to pray about. You also need to know that there are some things you just can't fix. No matter how hard we try as humans to make everything right and just, it's impossible."

"But doesn't God want us to be good and pure in our thoughts?"

"Yes, of course, He does. But it's not going to happen one

hundred percent of the time, and He knows it. That's why He sent His Son. Jesus was the only perfect man ever to walk this earth, and it's our job to worship Him and share the good news that He's saved us from our sin nature."

Shannon had a lot to think about. "I still want to help that man's family."

"Yes, of course you do. So do I. Fortunately, the Lord has placed a kind nature in your heart, and He's given us the ability to know right from wrong."

Shannon suddenly felt shame because she suspected he was talking about what the Lord did for believers, those who walked in His Word and knew scripture.

"I'm not so sure it has anything to do with my faith," she managed to sputter.

"There are kind people who don't believe in Jesus," Pastor Manning assured her. "The big difference between them and us is that we want to please Jesus, and we do kind things for people to His glory."

"Wow!"

Pastor Manning snickered. "Yeah, my sentiments exactly. I never cease to be wowed by all the goodness of God."

Two hours after Shannon walked into his office, she stood at the door getting ready to leave. He took her hands in his and said a short prayer for mercy and healing.

When she opened her eyes, he smiled. "Would you like for me to find someone to work with you? If you feel like you still need some help, I know a few people."

Shannon shook her head. "No, I don't think so. Not now, anyway. You've made some things very clear to me. Now I need to go home and do some serious thinking."

"And praying," he added.

"Yes, and praying and studying my Bible."

"Oh, just a minute. Let me get the tracts I subscribe to."

He quickly moved over to his file cabinet, flipped through some papers, and came back with a pamphlet in his hands. "This one deals with understanding why bad things happen in this world and allowing the Lord to work through them."

"Thank you so much, Pastor Manning. You don't know how much you've helped."

"I can't take credit for any of it," he replied, pointing his finger heavenward.

Shannon hurried down the hall toward the exit, when suddenly, a familiar figure stepped out from a darkened room. "Judd! What're you doing here?"

six

"I thought I'd stop by to see Uncle Garrett."

Shannon lifted one eyebrow. "Really?"

"Well. . ."

"Level with me, Judd."

He rolled his eyes and slapped his forehead with the palm of his hand. "You caught me."

Shannon glanced at her watch. "Shouldn't you still be in school?"

"Teacher in-service day. Kids aren't in school, so when the workshops are over, we're dismissed."

"Well, good for you."

Shannon took a step back and watched as Judd's expression changed from contrition to calculating. She loved the way he let his feelings show. He'd make a lousy actor. . .or model, which was good.

"Since I'm here, and you're here," he said slowly, "how about doing something together this afternoon?"

"Sounds good, but I can't."

"Why not?"

Disappointment shrouded Shannon. "I wish I could, but I have plans."

"Oh." He glanced down and shifted his feet. She saw how his expression changed once again. Disappointment and worry had taken over.

"With my mom," she said.

"Oh," he said again, only this time, a smile covered his lips, and he looked at her. "In that case, don't let me keep you."

As they parted, Shannon felt like she was walking on air. Seeing Judd always did that to her. He wasn't nearly as handsome as Armand by most women's standards, but he looked much better to her. More real. More animated. He never minded showing his feelings. And while Armand worried about getting lines from smiling, that concept never seemed to worry Judd in the least.

Shannon was still nervous about driving, but she'd been forced to venture out more. She couldn't very well expect other people to drive her everywhere she needed to go, so she tightened her jaw and moved ahead, forcing herself to deal with life. Her inborn streak of independence had returned.

No matter how much she talked to herself about how safe the back roads she took were, by the time she got to her parents' house, her hands were shaking, her palms were sweaty, and her head ached. When would this fear ever end? Or would it?

The neighborhood hadn't changed much since she lived here, with the exception of the trees, which had grown a few feet taller. The long driveway, which led to the garage in the back of the house, was shaded by oaks with branches that overhung the concrete path, almost like long, sheltering arms protecting the people who'd arrived.

Shannon took her time, allowing the scents to fill her nostrils and the sounds to bring back memories. The back-facing garage door was open, exposing both of her parents' cars, parked side-by-side as they had been for as long as she could remember.

"I've been worried about you, Shannon," her mother said first thing. "I was afraid you wouldn't make it. You're late."

"Just by ten minutes," Shannon reminded her, defending herself.

"We can't keep Cissy waiting. You know how busy she is.

When you have the best hairdresser in town, you have to be there early. She's booked into next month, you know."

"Yes, I know. You keep reminding me."

"Don't get sarcastic, Shannon."

Just then, her father rounded the corner, his arms extended, a wide smile on his face. "Shannon, baby, come give me a hug."

"Daddy. Why are you home this early?"

Shannon noticed her parents exchanging a glance before her mother ushered her out the door. "C'mon, let's go. We can't dilly-dally any longer."

"I need to talk with you about something later," Shannon told her dad. Then she turned to her mother. "Want me to drive?"

Her mother paused, then nervously flicked her wrist toward her own car. "No, I'll drive. We don't have much time."

Shannon wasn't sure if her mother was being polite or if she didn't trust her driving. Whatever the case, Shannon didn't argue. As always, she went along with her mother to keep the peace.

The woman was white-knuckled as she maneuvered the oversized luxury car through the streets of the Atlanta suburbs, her gazed fixed on the road ahead. She was on a mission. They were halfway to the hairdresser her mother had picked after interviewing a two-page list. Cissy, the hairdresser, had a clientele that impressed her, so that's who she insisted Shannon choose. Being the dutiful daughter she was—or not wanting to make waves because she couldn't stand the repercussions—Shannon had agreed to this awkward time for her hair appointment.

"I'm curious about something," Shannon said.

"If you have questions, just ask," her mother snapped. "Don't beat around the bush."

"What's going on between you and Daddy?"

"I don't know what you're talking about, Shannon."

Her expression was guarded, but her grip on the steering wheel grew even tighter. Shannon knew she'd hit a nerve.

"I saw that look you gave each other."

There was a long silence. Shannon studied her mother, who was trying to focus on her driving but was clearly distressed. Whatever the problem was, Shannon suspected her mother wasn't ready to discuss it.

"We've been married nearly thirty years. We do look at each other occasionally."

Shannon could tell it was no use to press any further, but her radar was up. She was determined to find out why her parents were acting so odd. After she'd left the hospital, she'd only seen her father once, and that was very briefly, before her mother had almost pushed him out the door.

"Here we are," her mother said as she quickly swung the car into the parking space of a strip mall. "Better hurry."

Shannon glanced at her watch. "We're not that late. I'm sure she's used to waiting a few minutes for some of her clients."

Cissy stood tapping her foot with a scowl on her face. "You're late," she said sternly.

"I'm so sorry," Shannon's mom apologized. "It won't happen again."

"I'm booked tight, you know."

"Yes, I'm fully aware of that. My daughter's still dealing with the fear of being in a car. This isn't easy for her."

Shannon watched the two women as they looked at each other with understanding. She decided right then and there that she'd find another hairdresser before the next time she needed a trim. No way would she grovel for being just a few minutes late—especially when the hairdresser had such an uppity attitude. Even as a supermodel, Shannon never spoke to anyone with the haughty attitude Cissy had.

Shannon sat in the chair while her mother gave orders to Cissy, explaining what she wanted, which wasn't what Shannon wanted at all. Finally, before Cissy's scissors were anywhere near her hair, she stood up from the chair and turned around to face her mother.

"Stop right now. I'm not five years old."

"Oh, sit down, Shannon. You've been through a lot lately. I'm just trying to help."

"Maybe so, but I don't want my hair looking all fussy. I don't have time to take care of anything elaborate." Turning to Cissy, she added, "Just take an inch off the ends. That's all."

A look of disapproval flitted across Cissy's face as she glanced at Shannon's mother, who shrugged.

"Well?" Cissy asked.

Her mother let out a heavy breath of exasperation. "Just do what she says. It's taking a little longer to get over it than I thought."

Cissy lifted the scissors with one hand and pushed Shannon back down into the chair with the other. "Whatever. But next time you come here, you need to let me tell you what you need."

There won't be a next time, Shannon thought as she stiffened with anticipation over having her hair trimmed. She watched closely to make sure Cissy did as she was told. The last bad haircut she'd had took months to grow out, and that involved wearing hats and tons of hairspray, which she hated.

When the ordeal was over, Shannon managed to beat her mother to the front desk. She pulled out a wad of bills, but her mother was even faster, shoving money into Cissy's pocket before Shannon had a chance to pay.

Shannon tried to swat at her mother's hand to keep her

from paying. "I have plenty of money, Mom. You don't need to pay my way."

They glared at each other, while Cissy stood there, waiting, for the first time showing patience. Shannon won the battle as she shamed her mother into backing off.

"Don't embarrass me like that again," her mother said as they got in the car.

Shannon sat, tight-jawed, forcing herself to remain quiet. She wasn't in the mood to argue.

Her father was waiting for them when they got back to her parents' house. "You don't look any different," he said with a chuckle. "And I bet you paid a fortune to stay the same."

Shannon's mom made some unintelligible sound as she stormed past him and headed for her room. He winked at Shannon.

"Hey, Dad, what's up with you two?"

"Nothing with me, but I think your mother's been suffering from empty-nest syndrome since you've been gone."

"I've been gone a long time."

"And your mother's been acting like this the whole time."

They exchanged a look of understanding during a moment's silence. Suddenly, Shannon remembered her idea about helping the family of the man who'd hit her. When she told her dad, his face lit up.

"I'd love to help. Where do they live?"

"North Carolina," Shannon said.

"That's a long way for me to go."

"I know, but I'll rent you a hotel room if you're willing to do it."

"You don't need to pay my way, Shannon. It'll be my pleasure."

"Okay, then, I'll send money for their bills," she said. "Even if he had life insurance, I'm sure every little bit will help."

Nodding, her father agreed. "You're right."

Shannon chatted with him for a few minutes over coffee before she stood. "I really need to go home now. The stress of driving totally wears me out."

He walked her to the door, where they hugged. "You turned out to be quite a woman, Shannon," he said. "I'm very proud of you."

All the way home, she thought about her mother's mood and realized there was something else going on. Depression, maybe? Whatever it was didn't look good.

When she got home, her answering machine light was blinking. The first call was from Janie. The second was from Judd.

She called Janie first.

"You are going to the Bible study, aren't you?" Janie asked.

"I'd like to, but after what happened last time I was there, I'm not sure I should show my face."

"Don't be silly. Of course you should go."

"They're going to think I'm a complete nerd for acting like I did."

"So? We all act nerdy sometimes. Get over it."

Shannon laughed. "Well, I guess I do have to face people sooner or later."

"Yeah, and what better place than where we're all studying God's Word?"

Judd had called to ask if she wanted a ride to the Bible study. "I wasn't sure if you wanted to go alone, with Janie, or if I could take you."

"Would you like to take me?" Shannon asked.

"I'd love to."

"Okay, then it's a date."

The second she said that, she felt like kicking herself. It wasn't a date. It was just a ride to the Bible study.

"Sounds good," Judd said.

At least he hadn't made an issue of her faux pas. Shannon decided she needed to be more careful with what she said from now on.

When Judd arrived, he looked her over, but he didn't say a word about her appearance. She'd spent quite a bit of time getting ready, so she was a little disappointed.

All the way to the church, Shannon chattered about getting her hair trimmed and seeing her parents. He listened but didn't say more than an occasional "mm-hmm" and "that's nice."

A few people were scurrying around, moving chairs, and getting the refreshments ready. A few of them stopped and hugged her, saying it was good to see her.

"Good to see you back," Paul said as he came up to her. "How're you feeling?"

"Much better."

Everyone in the room approached her at some point, both before the Bible study began and during the break. They were all concerned about her, and they expressed their gratitude that their prayers had been answered.

All the studying she and Judd had done paid off. Not only did she understand everything they talked about, she participated as much as anyone else. With each comment, she felt more a part of the group. During the social time, when they talked about what was going on in their lives, Judd shared that he'd had a particularly rough day at school with some behavior problems. Shannon was relieved that she hadn't caused his bad mood.

When it was her turn, she talked about how she was overcoming her fear of driving. They all promised to continue praying for her recovery—mental, physical, and emotional.

She appreciated all they were doing. And she didn't doubt their sincere concern. The only problem was, she wasn't sure if she truly felt God's message like everyone else did. Was she just giving lip service, or did she actually "get" it?"

On the way back to her place, Judd stopped at a light and turned to her. "Something's bothering you. Wanna talk about it?"

Shannon shrugged, thinking she'd be better off not discussing her doubts. After all, what good would it do to question the very fiber of what he believed in?

"Not really."

"Okay, if you're not ready, that's fine. But I'm all ears if you change your mind."

He asked her if she wanted to stop off for coffee, but she turned him down. "I really need to get home. It's been a trying day for both of us."

That was true, but what she didn't tell him was that she'd been wrestling with her beliefs, until he'd picked her up. He let her off the hook for now.

Over the next several weeks, Shannon went through the motions of studying and bringing what she'd memorized to the Bible study. It appeared that she had everyone fooled—everyone, that is, but Judd. She knew it was only a matter of time before he said something.

"Something's going on with you," he finally told her one night after a long study session. "I'm sensing that you're not as into this whole Bible study thing as you want everyone to believe."

"Don't be silly," she replied.

He gave her one of his looks, reached out, and squeezed her hand. Then he hopped out of the car and ran around to her side to open her door. Shannon liked that about him—the fact that he was such a gentleman. Armand had been nice and polite, but it had never dawned on him to hold doors or let her go first. But then, he hadn't grown up with parents who'd taught him to be a gentleman. He came from a long line of jet-setters, which meant he'd been raised by a series of nannies.

That night, after she got home, she decided she needed to do some serious soul-searching. If she planned to continue with the Bible study, she felt like she owed it to everyone there, including herself, to believe the words that came out of her mouth.

First thing she did was call Janie. It was hard, but she confessed what had been plaguing her.

"I could tell something was wrong," Janie said sympathetically. "Why don't you venture out and find some scripture that speaks directly to you?"

"Where do I start?"

"Do you still have that concordance I brought over?"

"Yes, that's what I've been using."

"Then start with the word *faith*, and go from there."

"Okay, I'll give it a try."

"Don't forget to open and close with prayer. Ask the Lord to show you what you need. He listens."

"Thanks, Janie," Shannon said softly. She knew she could count on her best friend.

Shannon looked up all the verses listed in her concordance. She read Job chapter nineteen, verse twenty-five, and silently pondered the message about how it related to faith. Then, she moved on to Isaiah chapter twelve, verse two, which dealt with trusting the Lord. But it was the ninth chapter of Mark that really touched her heart, especially the twenty-fourth verse, when the demon-possessed child's father said, "I do believe; help me overcome my unbelief!"

Shannon thought about how she could relate to that situation. Until Janie had dragged her to the Bible study, she'd been caught up in worldly ways, which didn't appear evil on the surface. It was much subtler, but the gentle tugs away from God's Word had been there. The fame, the fortune, and the shallow relationship she'd had with Armand had been veiled attempts by Satan to pull her away from what was truly important in her life.

An incredible feeling of understanding washed over Shannon. Although she knew she still hadn't gone deep enough into the gospel message for a true understanding, she knew the Lord was speaking to her through His Word. Janie had been right. All she had to do was look to the only true message in this world, and the answers would be there.

The following week, she got a little behind on the Bible study lesson because she'd taken a side trip in her own studies. However, no one seemed to mind that she didn't participate. She listened attentively and made up her mind to get back on track with everyone else.

Each week that passed brought more strength of conviction to Shannon. She did her lessons and allowed herself to get sidetracked to other verses when she needed a better understanding. If something wasn't clear, she looked it up in the concordance. And then, if she couldn't find what she needed, she called Janie, even though she didn't always have answers.

"You might want to call Pastor Manning. He's a very wise man."

Judd had backed off to give her space, which she appreciated. However, she missed the warmth of his friendship and the way he made her feel inside.

He still hadn't rushed her or made an issue of her external beauty. In fact, after the first couple of comments about her looks, he hadn't said a word about them.

As much as she appreciated the space, Shannon couldn't stand it anymore. She finally picked up the phone and punched in Judd's number. His answering machine picked up after the fourth ring, so she left a message.

Two hours later, he called her, panic evident in his voice. "You called?"

"Yes, I was wondering if we could get together and study. You know, like we used to."

"Is everything okay?"

"Yes, everything's fine. Why?"

He blew out an audible breath. "Oh, man, you had me worried. Your message said it was urgent and to call as soon as possible."

She hadn't thought about how her message would sound, but she had wanted to talk to him soon. "I'm really sorry, Judd. It's just that when I get my mind set on something, I don't like to waste time."

"Don't worry," he said. "Why don't we meet somewhere?"

"I thought we could study here."

"Maybe it would be better if I met you somewhere, like halfway."

"Okay," she said slowly. His tone had changed, and it worried her.

❧

Maybe being out in public with Shannon would keep his mind off his feelings toward her. All Judd had been able to think about since meeting her was how he was starting to fall head-over-heels for her. In fact, for the first time in his life, he understood what it meant when people said they'd "fallen" in love. That was exactly how he felt—like he'd fallen and couldn't get up.

They made arrangements to meet at the Dunk 'n Dine, at her suggestion. "For old times' sake," she'd said. "We can eat pancakes until they're coming out our ears."

Judd concentrated hard on the current week's Bible study. He took turns with Shannon, looking up the answers. She smiled often, and he had to restrain himself, when all he wanted to do was reach across the table and touch her.

At the end of the lesson, they agreed to meet weekly, since they were at the same level of understanding. Shannon hesitated, looking at him with questioning eyes, but she didn't ask anything as she turned to leave. He felt like a piece of his heart left with her.

Over time, Judd was able to be around Shannon and still focus on the Bible study lesson, but there were times when their hands brushed and he got a tightening sensation in his chest. It was a feeling of anticipation, of excitement, and of wondering if the other person felt it, too.

Something else Judd had noticed was that Shannon's scar had begun to fade. In fact, he had to look hard to see it, and the only reason he could was because he knew it was there. He wasn't sure she was aware how it had almost disappeared, because she still, on occasion, touched her cheek with her fingertips. He wanted to reach out and cover her hand with his, but he didn't dare.

Judd delighted as Shannon's faith grew and she became more confident in her knowledge of scripture. She had become bolder in speaking up about her faith, and when they had new members or visitors, she was often one of the first people to greet them. She didn't hesitate to speak out about her newly discovered faith, and when they were in the question-and-answer part of their study, she spoke out as often as anyone else in the room. That also quickened Judd's heart. He loved watching the transformation. He also knew that Shannon was responsible for his own faith growing to the level where it was. She'd challenged him by asking questions, making him study harder, and proving that a person could come from rock bottom to the top by allowing Jesus to touch her heart. Jesus had worked a miracle in both of them, something Judd was grateful for.

"I have something special to discuss with you next time we get together to study," Shannon said as they walked out to the church parking lot together. "I know you like to go to the Dunk 'n Dine, but I was wondering if we could study at my place."

Judd thought for a few seconds before nodding. "Sure. That would be fine." After all, he'd gotten used to the feelings she never ceased to awaken in him. He could manage the heart palpitations at her place as much as he could at the Dunk 'n Dine, couldn't he?

❧

The first thing he noticed when she yanked open the door was the twinkle in her eye that showed her mischievous side. She was up to something, he could tell.

The instant he sat down, she plopped into the oversized chair across from him, tucked her legs under herself, and leaned forward. "We need to talk," she said.

Judd gulped. What had he done now?

"Okay," he said slowly, almost wishing they were at the Dunk 'n Dine rather than her cozy living room. "What's on your mind?"

"I've got all this time on my hands, and I'm starting to get antsy. I feel like I need to do something."

"Any thoughts about what?"

She shrugged. "I've thought about getting a job, but there's not much I'm trained to do."

"You could always go back to modeling."

On cue, her hand flew up to her cheek as she shook her head. "No, I don't think so."

"Any other ideas?"

"Since I have a little money stashed away, I don't have to get a job. Not yet, anyway. I was sort of thinking I might want to volunteer. I'd like to help others."

Judd smiled. He loved how Shannon thought about other people. Janie had told him how she'd sent money to the family of the man who'd crashed his car into hers. He was amazed at her ability to forgive and show compassion for those less fortunate.

"Any idea what you'd like to do?"

She made a funny face as she shook her head. "That's the problem. I don't even know where to start. What does a former model know how to do that can help society?"

"I'm sure there are lots of things. Why don't we start with your gifts?"

"Janie told me to look in Romans chapter twelve. I think my gift is serving."

"I can see that," Judd said.

He'd noticed how quickly she volunteered to help out when someone was needed to deliver food to homebound members of the church. And she didn't hesitate to visit people in the nursing home.

"I think you're also an encourager," he added.

"You think so?"

"Yes, I do."

"Funny you should say that. Janie told me the same thing. Okay, now what do I do?"

"I'm not sure."

"What do you think your gifts are, Judd?"

"Well, I am a teacher, and it seems like a good fit. The kids in my classes are all doing well, and they're pretty happy—most of the time, anyway."

Shannon nodded. "I have no doubt teaching is one of your gifts. You know, I think you might be an encourager, too."

"Hmm. I never thought about being anything other than a teacher," he said.

"Look at it this way. You encouraged me to keep going to the Bible study. You encourage people in the group to participate. And one of the reasons you're such an effective teacher, I bet, is that you encourage the kids to be the best they possibly can."

"Good point."

Shannon lifted her hands and let them fall back to her lap. "Now what?"

"I guess we should figure out where we fit best."

"We?" Shannon asked, her head tilted to one side.

"Yes, we. I'd like to volunteer, too."

"Are you just saying it because that's what I want?"

"No. I'll admit you thought of it first, but I have time and the desire to help others, too."

A slow grin took over Shannon's face. "It'll be wonderful to do something together, Judd." She jumped up, crossed over to where he sat, and threw her arms around him. "You always know the answers."

"Not always," he argued as he tried to squirm away from her warmth.

She leaned back and gave him a puzzled look.

"For me, you do. Whenever I'm stumped, you always come through for me."

She'd pulled away from him a little more, but he could still feel her closeness. The urge to reach out and touch her was too strong to resist. Tentatively at first, he touched the side of her face with his fingertips. Then, slowly and deliberately, he slid his hand to the back of her head, his fingers getting caught in her tangle of long, blond hair. Her eyes widened as he pulled her to him for a kiss.

❧

Shannon's breath suddenly felt shaky. She'd kissed Armand countless times, but he'd never had this effect on her. But then again, Judd's kiss had so much more meaning than any of Armand's kisses ever had.

"I'm sorry, Shannon," Judd said as he suddenly let go of her. "I shouldn't have done that."

She struggled to find her voice. "Don't be sorry. I liked it."

"You did?"

Nodding, she had to swallow to find her voice again. "Yes. Very much."

He grinned. "Knowing that makes me happy."

Shannon wasn't sure if he had any idea how she felt. He'd distanced himself pretty quickly after the kiss—almost as if he was afraid to stay close to her.

After Judd left, Shannon leaned against the wall. Something significant had just happened, and she wasn't sure what to do about it. That one simple kiss had changed things between them. He'd kissed her before, but the emotion behind this was incredible. She wondered if he felt it, too.

As the minutes ticked by, and then the hours, feelings of doubt began to take over the excitement of the kiss. What if he'd only meant it as a gesture of friendship? Or perhaps he didn't mean anything at all. Which would be worse? Given the fact that she thought she might be falling in love, neither appealed to her. She wanted him to care as much for her as she did him. The very thought of her love being one-sided sent her heart into a free fall and then landed in a giant thud.

Shannon wasn't sleepy, so she decided to do a little channel surfing, hoping to make her eyelids heavy. When the phone rang, she glanced up at the clock. Who could be calling at this hour?

seven

"Shannon?"

"Judd? It's late."

"Were you sleeping?"

She paused before replying, "No, I was watching TV."

"I've been thinking."

"So have I," Shannon quickly replied. "What were you thinking about?"

"You tell me first."

"No, you called me."

She heard him inhale before clearing his throat. "I was thinking about what you said."

She thought for a moment and tried to remember anything she said that would elicit a late-night phone call. "What did I say?"

"You were saying you wanted to do something constructive with your life. I've got some ideas."

"Is that what you were thinking about?"

"Yeah, how about you? It's your turn."

Shannon briefly pondered letting him know what was really on her mind, but she figured it was best left unsaid. "Nothing, really. My mind was racing about everything, and I wouldn't even know where to start."

"I'm patient. I'm also a good listener."

"Yes, I know, but we can talk about that later." Shannon sucked in a breath, then slowly blew it out. "What ideas did you have for me?"

"Well, there are a couple of things the church is involved

in, plus some secular stuff downtown Atlanta."

Shannon thought for a moment. "What all is the church involved in?"

"One thing I think you might like is the 'Room at the Inn' program."

"Room at the Inn? What's that?"

Judd explained how the homeless shelters always filled up early, which left hundreds of families on the streets during the cold winter nights. Area churches coordinated sponsoring "Room at the Inn" nights, where they let homeless individuals and families stay in sanctuaries, fellowship halls, and classrooms. People from each church provided meals, clothing, and messages about Christ's love.

"Sounds wonderful," Shannon replied. "I'd love to get involved. What do I need to do?"

"Uncle Garrett told me about it. I think our church has a turn coming up in a few weeks. I'll find out who's coordinating it."

"Let me know, okay?"

"Sure thing," Judd replied. "How're you feeling?"

"You were here just a little while ago. You saw me."

Yes, Judd saw her. That was for sure. He saw her long, blond hair flowing freely around her face, her sparkling eyes lighting up as they discussed anything and everything.

"Judd?"

Shaking himself back to the moment, Judd said, "I'm getting tired. I just wanted to call and make sure you were okay."

"Yes, I'm fine."

As they hung up, Judd thought about the real reason for his call. After he left her apartment, all he could think about was the kiss. It still lingered on his lips. He doubted he'd get any sleep, thinking about Shannon and how she affected him.

This wasn't supposed to be happening. Judd had plans,

which didn't include falling for a woman—at least not yet. He'd just started to get his feet on the ground, and he wanted to do a few things for himself before meeting someone he could get serious with.

Who was he kidding? Getting serious with Shannon McNab would be like trying to grab a star with his bare hands. It would be impossible and way too much for him to handle. Women like Shannon didn't fall for men like him.

He ran his tongue over his lips and tried to force her out of his mind. He'd be much better off staying away from her, but he knew it would be impossible. All she had to do was call, and he'd be there for her.

The week went by quickly for Judd, due to the reading fair he was hosting at the school. He barely had time to do the exercises in the workbook to get ready for the Bible study.

Shannon was at the church when he first arrived, getting the coffee ready. "I tried calling you," she said as she glanced over her shoulder. "You're never home anymore, and you didn't pick up your cell phone."

"Sorry," he said, hovering a few feet away. "I've been busy."

"That's what I thought. Janie came over, and we went over the lesson."

Suddenly, Janie stuck her head in the door. "Did someone say my name?"

Shannon chuckled. "Were you eavesdropping?"

"Yes." Janie came all the way into the room, carrying a tall box that was obviously heavy.

"Let me get that," Judd said as he quickly moved to her side.

As Janie tried to hand Judd the box, she tripped over the place where the carpet met the tiled floor, and the box fell with a loud bang before Judd could get a grip on it.

Janie gasped and all eyes quickly turned to Shannon, who stood there, stunned for a few seconds. Shannon's heart raced, but she was okay. She slowly allowed a shaky smile as she moved toward Janie.

"I'm so sorry," Janie said as she reached out to Shannon. "You okay?"

Shannon glanced over at Judd, who stood with his hands in his pockets, watching her, concern evident in his expression. But he wasn't making a move toward her. It was as if he wasn't sure what to do.

"I'm fine. It scared me, but nothing like before. I think I'm starting to heal on the inside."

Janie, Judd, and the couple of people who'd drifted into the room let out a collective sigh of relief.

The Bible study was brief, since everyone seemed to be in a hurry. Judd darted out of the fellowship hall before Shannon had a chance to chat with him. Janie eyed her but waited until Judd was gone to approach.

"Wanna do something, since we're out early?" she asked.

Shannon nodded. "Sounds like a good idea."

"How about a snack?"

"I'm putting on a bunch of weight."

Janie's gaze raked her from head to toe, but she didn't say anything.

"A snack sounds good," Shannon finally said after an uncomfortable silence. "Where do you want to go?"

Janie shrugged. "How about the Dunk 'n Dine?"

Shannon paused, thinking about how she and Judd liked to go there. She'd begun to think of that as their place, but that was silly.

"I'll meet you there in fifteen minutes. I need to help clean up here first."

"You can go on," Paul said. "I can finish up here."

"No, I want to help."

Paul handed her a broom. "You're a good woman, Shannon. I hope you decide to stick around. We like having you being part of the group."

"I like it here, too," she said with a smile.

"Oh, and before you leave, there's a wet rag on the table. If you don't mind—"

"I'll wipe everything off before I leave," she said before he got the words out.

"I need to run this coffee urn to the kitchen, then I'm outta here."

"See you next week, Paul."

When Shannon finished cleaning the meeting room, she went straight to the Dunk 'n Dine, where she saw Janie waiting at a booth toward the front. Good. At least she wasn't in the back, where Judd liked to sit.

"We need to talk," Janie said the second she sat down.

"You don't waste any time, do you?"

"No, I try not to. What's going on between you and Judd?"

Shannon pulled her bottom lip between her teeth as she thought for a moment. "I wish I knew."

"What happened? Did you have an argument?"

"No, he came over one night last week, and suddenly, he acted like someone had bitten him on the foot. One minute we were talking about what I should do with the rest of my life, he kissed me, and than suddenly, he couldn't wait to leave."

"Wait a minute. Slow down." Janie leaned toward her, her eyebrows pulled together in a tight line. "He kissed you?"

Shannon smiled and nodded. She felt as shy as she had in junior high when Bobby Anderson had told everyone he loved her.

"Yeah."

"You never told me."

"It was just a kiss."

"With guys like Judd, it's never just a kiss. Maybe you're used to faster men, but in our crowd, guys don't kiss women unless they mean it."

"I know," Shannon admitted. "That's what makes it so strange."

"And what's this talk about what you want to do with the rest of your life? Are you planning something I should know about?"

Leave it to Janie to know where to dig, and then get right to the point. She was smart, and she wasn't the type to leave anything alone.

"I feel like my life doesn't have meaning. Judd was trying to help me figure out where to go from here."

"Somehow, I don't think Judd's the type to tell you what to do. Have you come up with any ideas?"

"I think I might like to do some volunteer work."

"Volunteering is good. Any thoughts about where?"

"Judd mentioned something about Room at the Inn."

"That's a good start," Janie said, "but it's only for one week a year. That's an excellent ministry, though, so it's a worthwhile thing to do. Gretta coordinates it. I'll tell her you're interested."

"I haven't thought about what to do besides that."

"You're a very talented woman, Shannon."

"Only when it comes to fashion. But somehow, I don't know if I can figure out how to work fashion into a ministry."

"You want to do something in the ministry?"

"I'm not sure yet. I thought I might."

"Look, Shannon," Janie said as she fidgeted with her napkin, "I don't want to discourage you from doing the Lord's work. But you've only recently started studying the Bible. There are many ways you can put your talents to work that will please God. All work, if done to His glory, can be a ministry."

Shannon listened to the wisdom of Janie's words. "I just don't know where to start."

"Why don't you go back to school? Remember how you always said you'd like to work with animals?"

"That was a long time ago. I'm not sure if I'm up to going back to school."

"You don't have to go full-time until you're ready. I do think you should sign up for one class next semester. It would get you out, and you can explore options."

"I'll have to think about it."

"In the meantime, if I come up with any brilliant ideas, I'll let you know."

Shannon smiled at Janie, knowing she would have more than one brilliant idea. She always did. Janie had always been the type of friend who didn't let up. If there was a problem, she set out to solve it, and she didn't quit until she'd accomplished her mission.

After she ate her salad, Shannon went to her apartment. Judd had called and left a message, but it was too late to return his call. She knew he had to get up extra early for school because the book fair was still going on at the school. He put in long days for those kids, which endeared him to her even more. The man was so selfless that she felt small and insignificant next to him.

He called her the next day around noon. "I was worried about you last night," he said, not even bothering to identify himself.

"Janie and I went out for a snack after the Bible study."

"I'm sorry. I didn't mean for you to feel like you had to account for every minute."

"I didn't take it that way."

Shannon was actually flattered that he cared enough to worry.

"Good. I'd never want to do that to you."

"How's the book fair?"

"As much fun as it's been, and I feel bad for saying this, I'm glad it's almost over."

"You've put a lot of work into it."

"Yes," he said, "I have. At least I've documented everything that needs to be done, so next year it should be much easier."

A few seconds of silence filled the phone line before Shannon spoke.

"Would you like to come over soon?"

"To study?"

That wasn't what she had in mind, but she couldn't tell him she just wanted to look at him and hope for another kiss. "Yeah, to study."

He paused, allowing a feeling of concern to wash over Shannon. "Sure," he finally replied. "How about the day after tomorrow?"

"Sounds good."

She called Janie later because she'd promised to let her know if she talked to Judd. Why, she wasn't sure, but it seemed important to Janie.

"Remember he's not used to women like you," Janie reminded her.

"Women like me?"

"Yeah. Women who can get any man they want with the snap of her finger."

"That's silly. I've never snapped my finger at a man."

"Maybe not, but you could if you wanted to."

Shannon laughed out loud, but after hanging up, she thought about what Janie had said. It seemed odd that people would think that just because she was a model, deep down she was any different from the rest of the women in the world. Quite the contrary. Shannon had the same desire for love and acceptance anyone else had.

Her mother paid her a visit the next morning. "Shannon, honey, have you looked in the mirror recently?"

"Of course I have. I look in it every morning when I brush my teeth."

Gently nudging Shannon toward the bathroom, she said, "Go take a look at your cheek."

"What about my cheek?"

"The scar is almost gone. I can't believe it healed so well without surgery, but it looks like you were right."

As Shannon studied her cheek, she saw the reflection of her mother right behind her, an expectant look on her face. She spun around and faced her.

She opened her mouth to comment, but her mother interrupted her.

"I'm not saying you have to do anything right away, Shannon, but you might want to put in a call to your agent. Let her know it won't be too much longer before you can get back to work."

"I'm not sure if that's what I want anymore, Mom."

"That's ridiculous. Don't let a setback like this keep you from the career that was meant for you."

This was such a standard argument between them, Shannon knew it was pointless to continue. So she shrugged. "I'll think about it."

She didn't have to think too long. Her agent, Melinda, called her early the next morning.

"I spoke to your mother yesterday afternoon. She says you're almost ready to return. I'm sure all the accounts will be very happy."

Shannon listened as her agent chattered on and on about how she had big plans for Shannon's return to the business. She even planned to take advantage of the fact that Shannon had found peace through the spiritual guidance she'd gotten at her church.

"How did you know about that?" Shannon asked.

"Your mother told me you've become something of a religious zealot."

"That's a distortion," Shannon said. "I don't want you exploiting my faith."

"Whatever," Melinda said. "Just let me know when you're ready, and I'll make sure you come back with a splash."

Shannon sighed but didn't say anything.

"Oh—and congratulations on your scar healing. After talking to Armand, I didn't think it was possible."

Alarm bells sounded in her head. "You and Armand talked about me?"

"Yes, dear, he was very concerned about you. He said his biggest fear was that your modeling career was over for good. He told me the scar was very deep."

The scar on my face wasn't the only one that was deep, Shannon thought.

"It is deep, but not as deep as others."

"You have more scars?" Melinda asked, sounding distressed.

"None you can see."

"That's good. I can hardly wait until you're ready to return, Shannon. You'll come back bigger and better than before. Sometimes it's good to take a little time off from the business. It stirs public interest."

That was the last thing Shannon cared about. Public interest. What was it, really? Just perception and nothing of any significance.

Shannon's mother started coming by the apartment every

afternoon. The first time, she was thrilled to have heard from Shannon's agent.

"Melinda called and asked when I thought you'd be ready to come back."

"Maybe never."

"Oh, don't be silly. You have to go back. What else will you do with your life? All you know is modeling. It's the only real job you've ever had."

Real job? Hardly. "I'm sure there's something else out there for me."

Shannon's mother stepped back, folded her arms, and shook her head. "Nothing else that can pay your bills, unless you go back to school for at least four years."

"I've got money in the bank," Shannon argued. "I don't need more than what I have."

"Then think about all the other people who depend on you. And how about the contracts you've signed? According to Melinda, you still have two years with the corn chip company, and the hair products company needs at least another year's worth of ads. And then there's. . ."

Shannon remained silent as her mother rattled off other companies and people who counted on her supermodel status. This was an angle she hadn't yet considered.

"Don't forget how Melinda has stuck her neck out for you. Remember, back when you were just getting started?"

Shannon nodded. How could she forget? Melinda had literally taken her by the hand and led her to her first audition. Then, when decision-making time came, she'd pulled all sorts of tricks to get Shannon her first television commercial. She'd taken chances—which had paid off big-time—but it could very easily have gone the other way.

"Melinda's agency is counting on you, Shannon. She's counting on you for her agency's survival."

Oh, man, her mother knew right where to hit.

"Yeah, you're right," Shannon finally agreed. "Looks like I need to do whatever I can to get back to work."

Next time Shannon saw Janie, she pointed to her face. "Do you see any trace of the scar?" she asked. "Be honest with me."

Janie narrowed her eyes. "Have I ever been anything but honest?"

"No, and that's why I'm asking you."

Taking a step closer and inspecting not only by looking but by reaching out and touching Shannon's face, Janie shook her head. "Looks to me like it's completely gone."

"Well, it's not completely gone, but it's faded enough to where I can hide it with makeup."

"That's great," Janie said. "You heal well."

Shannon managed a weak smile. "Yes, I'm very fortunate."

"So, what do you plan to do?"

With a brief lift of one shoulder, Shannon glanced away. "I haven't decided yet."

Janie groaned. "Don't tell me you're going back to modeling."

"It's a distinct possibility."

"Why would you wanna go and do that?"

"It's all I know how to do. Besides, my mother reminded me how my agent depends on me."

Janie snorted. "Don't give me that. There are plenty of things you can do."

"Name one," Shannon challenged. "And don't start talking about me going back to school."

"Okay," Janie agreed. "Since you don't need to work for money, you can do something that'll really help people. You've always cared about others. As for your agent, you know as well as I do, there are plenty of girls lined up waiting to take your place"

"I suppose you're right."

"Let's talk to the group about it after we finish the Bible study. I bet someone will come up with something."

"Good idea."

The next morning, Shannon's mother called, her voice laced with excitement. "I spoke to Melinda a few minutes ago. She's been lining up some things for you to do. We figured you could start back slowly and work you way into a full schedule."

"Don't you remember I'm not sure I'm going back?"

"I can't imagine why you wouldn't, Shannon."

"I've been thinking I might want to do something here."

"Modeling? Really, Shannon, you know New York's the best place for you. There's no way you can have a decent modeling career in Atlanta."

"No, not modeling. I was thinking about volunteering for a worthy cause. I really want to help people who aren't as fortunate as I've been."

"Let's discuss that later, okay?"

Shannon knew her mother needed time to think of an argument. "I really have to run now. I'm meeting Judd for lunch. He gets out of school early today."

"You're still seeing that schoolteacher?"

"We're friends." Shannon didn't think her mother would understand her feelings for Judd, so she didn't even try to explain them.

"Don't let this relationship get too tight," her mother warned. "I've heard Armand is coming back soon. In fact, he's been talking to Melinda, and he asked about you."

Shannon was surprised at how quickly she'd gotten over Armand. The initial shock over his departure had worn off in a matter of days, and now she realized her pain was more from injured pride than love lost.

Once she was off the phone, Shannon went into the

bathroom to put on her makeup. She studied her face in the mirror. As each day passed, her scar faded a little more. It was barely visible without makeup, and once she applied her foundation, it wasn't noticeable at all. The doctors had done an excellent job of stitching up her skin. Plus, she'd eaten very healthy food, taken plenty of vitamins, and gotten more rest than she ever had in her life.

When the phone rang, a sense of dread came over her. Hopefully, it wasn't Judd having to cancel.

It wasn't.

"Hey, Shannon, this is Melinda."

"Oh, hi."

"I'll pretend you didn't sound disappointed to hear from me," Melinda said in a voice that was a little too enthusiastic. "I just spoke to your mother. She said you want to do some charity work."

"Yes, I've been thinking about it."

"That's excellent. We have a whole list of opportunities here for celebrities to make a difference. This would provide excellent exposure for you in your comeback."

"I'm not doing it for myself," Shannon informed her.

"No, of course not. You're giving your time unselfishly. But why not capitalize on your kindness?"

Shannon started to tell her she needed to run, but Melinda kept going on and on about how much good she could do for underprivileged children all over the world if she participated in one of the world adoption programs. Then she started in on women's abuse shelters and how she'd already started talking to the woman who headed up the one in New Jersey.

"We have all sorts of wonderful things planned, Shannon. I guess I don't have to tell you I'm thrilled to have you back."

"Melinda, I really need to run now. I'm meeting someone in a few minutes."

"Okay, sweetie. Just remember, if you want to help others, it's always good to have greater means. If you stay there, you won't be able to help as many people as you can if you come here. Give me a call when you have more time."

After she hung up, Shannon glanced at the clock. She had to hurry so she wouldn't be late to meet Judd.

eight

One look at Shannon, and Judd knew something was wrong. Although she was smiling, pain clouded her eyes. There was something else, too. Confusion, maybe?

"Hungry?" he asked.

A brief look of panic shot across her face, then she shook her head. "No, not really."

"Why don't we go somewhere else, then. Wanna go for a walk?"

"Yes, that might be better."

Shannon had told him she was in the habit of keeping her running shoes in her bag from being in New York and having to run from one assignment to another early in her career. He waited while she changed from her dress shoes to sneakers.

"Always prepared, aren't you?" Judd asked.

"I try to be."

"So, what's on your mind?"

Judd forced himself not to look directly at Shannon. From being around her, he knew she had a hard time putting her thoughts into words when someone was staring at her.

"I'm still hung up on what I should do with my life. It's so hard."

"That can be really tough," he agreed. "What are your thoughts so far?"

Shannon slowed her pace to a crawl. "My agent called."

"Your agent?"

"Yeah, my modeling agent. She wants me back in New York."

"But I thought. . ." He turned to face her, and they both stopped. "I thought you wanted to stay here."

"I thought so, too, but I'm not sure now."

Judd felt like his heart had been yanked out of his chest. He was speechless. Suddenly, he felt the familiar shield he'd used growing up—the one that protected his heart against getting too close to people.

"My agent, Melinda, has some things lined up for me already. I told her I was thinking about doing some charity work, and she pointed out that I could do a lot more good for people if I went back to my old career."

"How does she figure that?"

"She said I can help homeless children and abused women all over the world because of my high visibility in modeling. If I don't go back, I'm limiting the good I can do."

Anger instantly welled in Judd's chest. It was obvious to him that her agent was playing with her emotions and taking advantage of Shannon's desire to be involved in a charity and to help others with her gifts. But he couldn't point that out to her now at the risk of sounding selfish. He wanted her here in Atlanta, and he suspected she knew that.

"Which way are you leaning?" he asked, trying hard to keep his anger from showing.

She lifted her shoulders, held them up for a few seconds, and then let them drop. "I'm still confused."

"Then I guess you'd better pray about it," Judd replied before correcting himself. "*We* need to pray about it."

He took a chance and looked directly into Shannon's eyes. It took every ounce of self-restraint not to grab her hands, pull her to him, and beg her to stay. But he knew he didn't have the right to keep her from following her dream. He'd gone after his, in spite of many people advising him to go into a higher-paying profession.

"Thanks, Judd. I wish the decision were easy. Nothing's clear to me."

"Sometimes the right thing isn't clear."

Or maybe it's clear and the selfish people in your life are trying to make it muddy. Judd was dying to yell those very words at her, but he held back.

"We'll just have to keep this in prayer and trust the Lord," Judd said, feeling like he was giving lip service to something he wasn't sure he believed at the moment.

"Yes, that's what we'll do."

When she left to go home, Judd felt an emptiness in his chest. But it wasn't nearly as painful as when she announced her dilemma to the Bible study group.

"It's a difficult decision," she said, "but the opportunity is there, and I feel like I at least need to consider it."

Everyone crowded around Shannon, talking over each other, promising prayers and best wishes. Judd remained on the sidelines as he watched, feeling like the ground had been pulled out from beneath him.

Janie cornered him in the parking lot.

"How can you let her even think about doing this?" she hissed.

"In case you haven't noticed, Shannon's a grown woman," he said.

"Do you love her?"

"What?"

"You heard me. Do you love her?"

Judd didn't want to risk sounding harsh, but Janie had no right asking such a question. "I think that's between her and me. I don't care to discuss it right now."

"I thought so," she said as she backed away. "You're gonna be sorry if you don't stop her, Judd. I know how Shannon lets people jerk her around. When her mother decided she needed to go into modeling to fulfill her own dream, she pushed Shannon into it."

"I'm sure Shannon didn't mind. She's done quite well."

"By the world's standards, yes, she's done great. But I don't think she's ever been happier than she's been since she started coming to church."

"Let's give her a chance to make up her own mind, okay?" Judd said.

Janie shook her head. "Like I said, you're gonna be sorry."

❧

"Melinda's right," her mother said. "Just think of all the things you can do when you go back. If you stick around here, you're so limited."

Shannon shook her head. "I've got such a great group of friends here, though. I never had this feeling in New York."

"You have friends everywhere. All over the world, thanks to your career."

"They're nothing like my friends here in Atlanta," Shannon said.

"Is there one in particular?"

What was the point in not being honest? "Yes, you know there is."

"I know you like this boy. What's his name? Judd? Whatever. I'm sure he's nice, but he's not Armand."

No, Shannon agreed. *He's not Armand, which is a good thing.*

"There are some wonderful churches up there, too. They're all over the place."

Shannon knew there were churches everywhere, so that wasn't an arguable point. "I really missed Janie when I was in New York."

"You'll see Janie when you come to visit us."

"It's not the same."

"But you can call her whenever you feel like talking. And

there's nothing stopping either of you from flying back and forth to visit. You make more than enough money to pay her way if you can't get down here."

This was another thing Shannon knew, but she also knew it wouldn't happen. When she'd first left, she and Janie planned trips and talked about it for hours. It happened a couple of times, but both of them got too busy to keep it up.

"We tried that, but it was too hard," Shannon said as she ran out of steam.

Finally, her mother drove the biggest point home. "You know all the sacrifices your father and I have made for you. This is something we've worked hard for. All parents want what's best for their children, and this is what we've worked toward all your life."

Shannon had argued in the past that modeling wasn't her life's goal, but then her mother had reminded her that all the classes, from modeling in junior high school to acting in high school, had prepared her for where she was today. Her mother even reminded Shannon that she hadn't been able to have her own career in order to concentrate on making a good life for Shannon.

"Let me think about it some more," Shannon agreed.

"Just don't wait too long. There are hundreds, maybe even thousands, of girls waiting to take your place. You know what a dog-eat-dog world it is out there."

Yes, Shannon did know about the kind of world it was out there—which was precisely the reason she doubted she wanted to jump back into it. Her life in Atlanta had begun to feel safe, and it made sense, unlike the insanity of the life she had in New York. Even her social life there was centered on her career. She had to be seen at certain events, which took all her free time. One of the reasons she and Armand had gotten so close was that they had the same obligations. They understood each other—or at least they thought they did.

A few days passed, and Shannon began to feel numb. Her mother's words had gotten to her. With the sacrifices her parents had made, how could Shannon have considered abandoning what they worked hard to achieve? All her own desires had to take a backseat to what her mother wanted for her. Was this how the Lord chose to answer her prayers?

She'd been asking for answers—no, begging. And her mother had been very clear in her message.

One morning, right after Shannon had finished going through her apartment, dusting and tidying the place, her doorbell rang. She cast a quick glance at the wall clock and wondered who it could be at this hour. The only person who didn't have a job with regular hours was her mother, and she was supposed to be at the club with some friends.

Shannon unbolted the door and pulled it open.

"Armand!"

Shannon felt as if her life had suddenly gone into freeze frame. The man she thought she loved, once upon a time, was standing at the door of her apartment, a bouquet of flowers in his arms and a wide, perfect smile on his lips.

She went numb, but only from shock. That flutter of the heart wasn't there.

"Mind if I come in?" he asked.

"Not at all," Shannon said as she stepped to one side.

He was dressed from head to toe in designer apparel, most likely that of one of the clients who paid him handsomely to show off clothes only the best-looking, perfectly shaped, chisel-featured men could carry off.

"You look fabulous, Shannon," he said as his eyes focused on her cheek.

"Other side, Armand," she said, turning her head and tapping the side of her face with her finger.

"Oh." His smile faded as he glanced at her other side. He abruptly looked away. "You've healed. . .nicely," he stammered. He quickly regained composure as he handed her the flowers. "For the most beautiful woman on earth."

"Thanks." She took them and turned toward the kitchen. "I'll put them in water. Have a seat."

It took Shannon a few minutes to stop shaking, so she didn't hurry with filling the vase. Why hadn't he called first? It wasn't cool for him to have shown up on her doorstep without some warning, at least.

When she got back to the living room, Armand was still standing, looking very uncomfortable. "Nice place," he said. "Something like this in New York would cost thousands of dollars a month."

Leave it to him to think of money. She'd noticed that about him before, and it hadn't bothered her. But now it did.

"It's not cheap, even by Atlanta standards," she said. "I like it."

"I understand you're thinking about coming back to work."

She looked him squarely in the eye without blinking. "Yeah, and I heard you've been talking to Melinda."

Armand shrugged as he darted his gaze away from hers. He wasn't a good liar, which made this very easy. It wouldn't take long to find out what his mission was.

"What's going on, Armand? Why are you here?"

Holding his hands out, he said, "I just wanted to see you, sweetheart. We've been an item for a long time, and I missed you."

"You missed me?" *Yeah, right.* She tossed him a crooked smile of disbelief as he squirmed.

"Yes, Shannon, I can't tell you how many sleepless nights I've had since your crash."

That sounded a little too rehearsed.

"I've had a few sleepless nights, too, Armand."

He came toward her, a look of genuine concern on his face. "Because of me?"

She shrugged. She didn't want to hurt his feelings, even after what he'd done to her. "Maybe."

"It was awful for me, too." His tone was a little tight, which she knew from experience meant he wanted something.

Now she couldn't hold back. "It must have been really rough at the chalet in Europe," she said, trying to mask the sarcasm.

"Harder than you can imagine."

"Oh, I can imagine, all right," Shannon said. She was amazed at how clueless Armand could be. "So what's the deal? Melinda sent you here to make sure I come back?"

He opened his mouth, snapped it shut, then snorted. "Okay, so Melinda did ask me to talk to you. But that doesn't matter. I've missed you, you've missed me, and that's all that counts."

"Actually, that's not all that counts, Armand," Shannon informed him. "I really did miss you at first, before I realized how little I meant to you."

He gasped. "That's simply not true, Shannon. You know I had to go to Europe for that photo shoot. You mean everything to me."

"What's your excuse for not calling?"

"You know how crazy the schedule is when you're busy working."

"Oh, yeah, the schedule." Shannon sometimes worked twenty hours a day, three days in a row, just so the photographers could get the light they needed for a single picture.

"It was awful."

"Who took my place?" Shannon asked. She just now realized she didn't know, and until now, it hadn't mattered. Amazing.

That should have been one of the first things she'd found out when she got out of the hospital.

"Patrice Hunt," Armand replied. "She felt terrible about what happened to you."

"I bet she did. Patrice has been watching every move I make for years, just waiting for me to mess up."

"That doesn't sound like you, Shannon."

Suddenly, she felt bad. *Catty* wasn't an adjective anyone had ever used to describe Shannon McNab. She'd been known as a playful, athletic, kindhearted girl who just happened to look gorgeous enough to be on magazine covers, television commercials, and designer runways.

"You're right, Armand," Shannon said remorsefully. "That was wrong of me. Patrice is a beautiful model who was the perfect replacement."

He reached for her. "I wouldn't say the perfect replacement. No one could ever take the place of Shannon McNab. You're the best model in the business."

Shannon pulled back and took a step away from Armand. She didn't want him touching her.

They stood and stared at each other for what seemed like forever. Armand took a tentative step toward her again, and she forced herself to stand still.

"I want you back, Shannon. I miss you something awful. Without you in my life, nothing seems real."

A shiver ran through her. His words made her want to turn and run out of her apartment, but she couldn't be rude. Armand hadn't done anything all that terrible.

"Where are you staying?" Shannon asked to avoid responding to his comment.

"The Hilton."

"Can we get together a little later in the day? I have someplace I need to be in about an hour."

"Sure, sweetheart. I just had to see you as soon as I got to town."

"Tell you what. I'll meet you in the lobby of your hotel at six. We can go somewhere for dinner and talk then."

"Sounds wonderful." Armand moved toward the door, graceful and fluid in the movement he'd learned from years of being one of the highest paid male supermodels. Shannon couldn't help but compare him to Judd, who took long, purposeful strides, his arms swinging dramatically by his side, like a man on a mission—not someone trying to sell something.

As soon as Armand left, Shannon threw on a dress, ran out to her car, and headed straight to the club where her mother played tennis and had lunch twice a week.

"Shannon!" the maitre d' shouted as she entered the main dining room. "It's been a very long time. You look lovely, dear!"

"Thanks, Maurice. Have you seen my mother?"

His smile quickly faded. "No, I just came on duty about fifteen minutes ago. Would you like for me to have one of the wait staff look for her?"

"No, that's not necessary. I can look for her, if you don't mind."

He gestured around the grand expanse of the room. "Be my guest, Shannon. You're always welcome here at my dining room."

"Thanks, Maurice. It was good seeing you."

"It's nice seeing you in person again. All these years of seeing you in magazines and TV, I feel like you never left. But you look much more beautiful in person."

As Shannon walked away, she chuckled to herself. Maurice was such a charmer, which was probably why he'd kept his job for so long. He'd been there since her parents first joined the club, back when she was in late elementary school.

There were half a dozen places where her mother could have

been. Passing through the snack bar, Shannon saw that she wasn't in there. It was a small area, with booths and counter stools all in a position to offer a nice view of one of the three televisions suspended from the ceiling.

The banquet room was dark, so she didn't bother checking there. That area was reserved for special occasions, like weddings, awards banquets, or birthday parties for overprivileged children. Shannon remembered the parties her parents had thrown for her in that very room—most of them forgettable. She always preferred small gatherings in someone's living room, with Pin the Tail on the Donkey. Her mother wouldn't have dreamed of doing something so simple and unsophisticated.

She had to ask around before she found her mother in the garden terrace, a green room filled with tropical plants and flowers that took a full-time staff to maintain.

"Shannon!" her mother exclaimed when someone alerted her that her daughter was behind her. She beamed at Shannon. "What a lovely surprise!"

With a tight face, Shannon glared at her mother. "Mom, did you know Armand was in town?"

The sincere surprise that registered on her mother's face told Shannon everything she wanted to know. "Why no, but how nice for him to come!" She turned to her friends. "Remember my daughter, Shannon McNab?"

All the women grinned at her. She offered them a clipped nod then turned back to her mother, who had a beatific expression that annoyed Shannon more than she cared to admit.

"Where is he?" She craned her neck. "Did you bring him with you?"

"Sorry to disappoint you, but no. I'm meeting him later for dinner at his hotel."

"You should have brought him," her mother said. "I'm sure these ladies would have loved to meet him."

"Yes, I'm sure."

"Well, I'm glad he came to see you, Shannon. See? He does love you. He's just been very busy lately, just like you'll be once you're back in the business you know best."

"Melinda must be fully responsible for this," Shannon muttered under her breath.

Her mother talked her into hanging around for lunch with the ladies. They all gushed and cooed over how beautiful Shannon was, and she smiled, accepting their compliments as gracefully as she could. But it was more of the same old adoring-her-for-her-beauty talk, making her very uncomfortable. The only time she could relax was when her mother told them how Shannon had talked her father into helping the poor family of the man who'd crashed into her. In fact, he was up in North Carolina now, working on some roof repairs.

"A good person as well as beautiful," one of her mother's friends said, sighing.

There it was again—another comment about her physical beauty. As soon as she could, she left.

Back at home, Shannon dialed Melinda's number. "Why didn't you tell me you were sending Armand?"

"He wanted to surprise you," Melinda said in her own defense. "The man's been pining over losing you, so I rearranged his schedule for the next several days."

"Pining over me?"

"Yes. You should see how he's been moping. I was worried the clients would notice, so I figured this would be the best thing for both of you."

"Hmm. Okay, if you say so." Shannon wasn't sure what to say next.

"You are coming back with him, aren't you?" The high-pitched sound of Melinda's voice grated Shannon's nerves.

"I'm not sure yet," Shannon admitted.

"I've got an idea. Why don't you come up here and give it a try? If you decide you don't like it anymore, fine. But at least you'll keep your place in the industry in the meantime."

"Keep my place?"

"Yes, dear. It's getting harder and harder to hold off the clients. They're all starting to wonder if something's seriously wrong with you."

"They know about the scar, right?"

"They know you were injured."

"What did you tell them?"

"I said you had some healing to do and that you'd be back as soon as you could. By the way, Armand says you look even more beautiful than before. He couldn't see even a trace of a scar on your face."

"He called you already?"

"Yes. Right after he left your apartment. You should have heard him. He was giddy with delight over seeing you. That man is completely and totally in love with you, Shannon. You're one very fortunate girl."

Shannon knew she should have been overcome with joy about the news, but she wasn't. Instead, she found herself wondering how Armand's feelings for her compared to Judd's.

As she got ready to see Armand, Shannon thought about how Armand had come all the way here to drag her back to New York. Judd, on the other hand, hadn't taken any steps to try to keep her in Atlanta. Even Janie had said she had to make the final decision herself. They'd all been praying for her, which was good. Maybe the answer to her prayer was Armand's surprise arrival.

After sorting through her jumbled thoughts, she made the decision on the way to see Armand to give modeling another try. Melinda had told her that was an option, and she didn't have to make a long-term commitment. She wouldn't sign any new contracts that would tie her down, so if she decided to go back to Atlanta, she could at any time.

As always, Armand was five minutes late. He didn't bother with an apology because punctuality wasn't in his vocabulary. This suddenly became a sore spot with Shannon, but she didn't say anything. Why had she put up with it for so long?

Throughout dinner, Armand worked on her, telling her about all the excitement in New York. Finally, she couldn't stand his sales job any longer, so she figured she might as well put him out of his misery.

"I'm going back, Armand."

"You're what?" he asked, stunned.

"I think you heard me. I'm going back to New York."

"This is wonderful news! Have you told Melinda?"

"I figured I'd call her first thing tomorrow."

Armand's eyes flickered with excitement through the rest of dinner. Neither of them ate dessert, but Shannon was dying for the chocolate cheesecake she knew the restaurant was known for. With a sigh, she resigned herself to living without desserts for as long as she remained in the modeling business.

By the time Shannon got back to her apartment, there was already a message on her machine. It was Melinda letting her know she had a test photo shoot scheduled for the following week.

Shannon knew that a test shoot meant they weren't sure she still had what it took. There was risk involved here, but she didn't feel the pressure like she once had. She'd done all this before, and it didn't matter to her any longer whether she succeeded or not.

Now all she had to do was tell her friends in Atlanta.

"Please don't go," Janie begged. "I tried my best to hold back, but I can't anymore. I think you're making a huge mistake."

"Why didn't you say something before?" Shannon asked.

"I thought you needed to make this decision without my interference."

"Since I've already committed to the photo shoot, I have to go. I'm still not sure that's what I need to do. It's only a test."

"Well, I hope you fail miserably."

Shannon laughed out loud. "Some friend you are."

"I'm the best friend you ever had," Janie said with a pout.

"You're right."

At the Bible study, when Shannon announced her big plans, Judd just sat there and stared at the wall. When the session was over, Shannon walked up to him and nudged his arm.

"You didn't say a word when I made my announcement."

He shrugged. "There wasn't much I could say."

"What do you think about me doing this?"

Judd reached down, took her hand, and held it as he looked into her eyes. Her heart stood still for a moment before he spoke.

"I think this is something you need to do, Shannon, if for no other reason but to find out if it's something you still want."

Suddenly, her heart fell with a thud. That wasn't what she wanted to hear.

nine

As Shannon left Judd, she felt empty, almost as if nothing really mattered anymore. And there was nothing to keep her in Atlanta other than her own desire to stay.

She'd expected her mother to be overjoyed, but she'd expected something completely different from Judd.

All the way to her parents' house the next morning, she braced herself for the smug satisfaction her mother was sure to show. She wasn't in the mood to deal with it, but she might as well get it over with.

"I would go with you, but I have commitments at the club," Shannon's mother said.

"Hey, don't worry about it. I'm a big girl. I lived alone in New York for years."

"I know, but this is such an important event for you, sweetheart. A turning point."

Yes, it sure was a turning point. But Shannon wasn't sure it was turning in the right direction.

"I'll be just fine. My old apartment still hasn't been leased, so I'll be able to stay there."

"I really think you should have taken Melinda up on her offer to find some roommates for you."

Shannon almost laughed at her mother this time. When she'd first moved to New York, her goal was to make enough money to move out of a crowded apartment with three other roommates. Her mother had done everything in her power to help her. And now she wanted her right back to where she'd started. No thanks. Shannon enjoyed the peace and quiet of her own place after a long day of being in front of cameras and crews who told her where to stand, what to wear, and how to look.

The time between announcing her decision and leaving went by in a blur. She stepped on the plane, hesitating for a moment as her insides lurched. Finally, she steeled herself, put one foot in front of the other, and found her seat. Why she'd bothered with booking a first-class seat was beyond her. As numb as she was, it was a total waste of money.

Melinda had a car waiting for her at LaGuardia. The driver, a stodgy middle-aged man with a frayed jacket and cap slightly resembling an old navy officer's uniform, held the door for her without uttering a single word.

He didn't wait for her to tell him where she was going before whisking her off toward Manhattan. He seemed to have a destination in mind, so she focused on the sights whizzing by.

She should have known. He pulled up in front of the mirrored building that housed the Glamour Agency, where Melinda and a few of her underlings held court. He promised to deliver her bags to her old apartment as he waited for her to go inside the building.

As she remembered, the lobby was crowded with dozens of young, fresh faces, all of them hopeful of having a career at least half as good as hers had been.

"There's Shannon McNab," she heard someone whisper.

"I don't think so," the girl next to her whispered. "I heard her face was burned beyond recognition in the car accident."

Shannon flashed her trademark smile. "Hi. I hope you girls get the contract of your dreams. Have a wonderful day."

Their eyes all widened as she breezed past them. "That *is* her," she heard as she went through the double doors without stopping at the receptionist's desk.

"Shannon!" shouted the agent in the front office. "Hey, everyone! Shannon's back!"

People came out of offices like bees out of a honeycomb, all of them hugging her and laughing with pure delight. Maybe this wasn't such a bad idea, after all. It felt good to get such a warm reception.

"Shannon!" Melinda said as she came out of her office, her arms open wide. "How wonderful to see you!"

"It's good to see you, too, Melinda." Shannon leaned over for the shorter woman to do her cheek-to-cheek greeting.

"Are you ready to get started?"

Shannon nodded. "I'm probably a little rusty, though."

Melinda flipped her hand from her wrist. "Nah. You'll do just fine. I've got several test shoots lined up."

She narrowed her eyes and studied Shannon's face.

"The scar's on this side," Shannon offered, tapping her left cheek and leaning forward.

Melinda's face lit up with delight. "I can't see it at all. Now we only need to wait and see what the camera tells us. The lighting they use will tell the whole story of your future in a second."

Shannon gulped. So that was what it all boiled down to.

Throughout the years she'd been modeling, Shannon hadn't deluded herself into thinking she'd get this much attention if she hadn't been beautiful enough to land such great modeling gigs. But she did feel like once people got to know her, they liked her for who she was deep down. However, the doubts continued to plague her—even now, seven months after Armand had walked away from her.

"Let's get moving, shall we?" Melinda had already started gesturing and motioning for her assistants to get back to their desks and get to work putting Shannon's career back in motion.

By the end of the day, Shannon was exhausted. The driver

dropped her off in front of the building she'd once called home. At least she knew where everything was.

The stark white furniture and light wood floors nearly blinded her when she walked inside and flipped on the light. She walked through the apartment and saw that everything had been cleaned for her homecoming. Melinda had thought of everything, all the way down to stocking her refrigerator with Shannon's favorite yogurt and bottled water.

Someone had unpacked her suitcases, which were lined up in the back of her room-sized walk-in closet. All she had to do for herself was eat a quick snack, change into her pajamas, and turn down the covers.

Sleep came easily for Shannon, as exhausted as she was. But when the alarm clock buzzed at five thirty, she was already awake. The sounds of the city had startled her from her sleep, and she hadn't been able to turn off the thoughts that had popped into her mind.

She met Melinda at seven to get her schedule. Then she let the driver take her around to get quick snapshots and fifteen- to thirty-second takes on film. In spite of how busy she was, images of Judd flashed through her mind, and she wondered what he was doing. Was he lecturing? Or was he spending time going over an assignment with one of the seventh-graders he cared about so much? She'd never known anyone like him before, and she doubted she ever would again.

Judd's suggestion about doing what she was called to do played over and over in her mind. Had the Lord sent Armand to her so she could go back to modeling? Or was this just temptation designed as a test? Whatever it was didn't feel right at the moment.

"Stop frowning, Shannon," the photographer said. "Where's that spark?"

"I'm sorry, Pete. I've sort of gotten out of the groove."

"Think happy thoughts. You and Armand strolling through Central Park."

Shannon took a deep breath and imagined herself with Armand. That doesn't do it, she thought as she felt her forehead growing tight. Then she remembered Judd's kiss.

"That's it, Shannon! You've got it, girlfriend!"

The quick clicking sounds of the camera were familiar to Shannon, bringing back all sorts of memories of France, Italy, and Spain. She'd spent several summers in Europe doing photo shoots and developing an international presence.

After three days of grueling photo and filming sessions, Shannon sank back on the sofa in Melinda's office. "Now what?" she asked.

Melinda shrugged. "Now we play the waiting game. We have to see how you do on film."

No matter how well known Shannon once was, in spite of how she'd recovered, her entire future modeling career hinged on lighting, cameras, and illusion. That very thought put a knot in her stomach.

Playing the waiting game didn't mean they sat back and did nothing. Melinda had arranged for Armand to escort Shannon to various functions, dropping hints in the media that he'd been by her bedside, worrying over her, being her motivation to get back to work. She even had the nerve to capitalize on Shannon's desire to help others who were less fortunate than her.

"I haven't done all this," Shannon growled at Melinda as she read the package put together for her new media campaign. "This article says I've been working with the homeless in Atlanta."

"You haven't yet," Melinda offered. "But you will. As soon as we get the results of the photos, we're setting up a homeless shelter with your name on it. It's such a brilliant move, I don't know why I didn't think of it before. In fact, I think I'll do it for all my top models in their hometowns." She leaned back in her chair and added, "Just think of what it'll do for your career."

This whole thing made Shannon sick to her stomach. Her motive hadn't been to help her career. She sincerely wanted to help people. And she wanted to do it because she felt like that was what Jesus wanted her to do.

The following week, Shannon noticed that Armand had suddenly disappeared from her itinerary. He'd been outwardly attentive to her lately, but she felt like they'd lost a deep personal connection. He smiled at all the right times, and he knew exactly when a camera was about to click. That was when he gazed lovingly into her eyes or gently placed his hand on her back to guide her as they walked to a celebrity function. It was all show and had no substance.

Life for Shannon was beginning to feel like an empty shell. Nothing had really changed. Why had she not seen this before?

"Where's Armand?" Shannon asked Melinda the morning they'd agreed to get together to go over the results all the photographers had sent by courier.

"He's getting ready to go back on the European tour," Melinda said as she stuck her letter opener in the envelope and started ripping.

"Isn't it a little early for that? They usually have the European tour during the summer, don't they?"

"You know how this business works, Shannon. We have to move schedules up all the time to get a head start on the competition."

Funny how Armand never mentioned he was leaving. If they were as close as the media said they were, surely they would have discussed his tour.

Deep down, Shannon didn't care. However, it did hurt her

pride. The whole thing with Armand was forced and awkward. It didn't feel right.

Being with Judd felt right.

Shannon blew out a sigh as Melinda read the reports. When she looked up with a twitching grin, Shannon knew the results were good.

"You're back in business, Shannon. Not a single camera saw your scar."

"Great!" Shannon replied, although she didn't feel as good as she hoped she sounded.

"No doubt you'll get contract-renewal offers from all the former clients. We'll have to review them and see if they're worthwhile. I'm also putting out some feelers for some new contracts."

"But why? If the old companies want me back, don't you think you should consider them first?"

Melinda glanced at her from above her glasses perched on the tip of her nose. "Bargaining power, Shannon. This business thrives on competition. People want what someone else has. That's how you make money in the image market."

The image market. That's what Shannon was in. It was all image. Illusion. Nothing real.

She slowly nodded. "I understand."

Melinda grinned. "Yes, I know you do. That's why you've done so well. You deliver what the client wants. Every woman wants to be you, Shannon. As long as we have that, you have a career in modeling."

How sad that people wanted her life when she wasn't sure she wanted it. Shannon stood and crossed the room to the door.

"One more thing, Shannon, before you leave."

Shannon stopped and turned to face Melinda. "What's that?"

"Armand is having an intimate get-together at Pierre's. Sort of a going-away party. He'll pick you up this evening at eight thirty."

Shannon nodded. All she wanted was to hang around in her apartment and read her Bible, but she knew she had to maintain this image thing Melinda had stressed from the moment they'd met.

On the way to the party that night, Armand turned to her, lifted her hand to his lips, and looked into her eyes. "Shannon, I'll be gone for a few weeks, but I feel that what we once had is worth bringing back."

She blinked as she stared back at him. He kissed her hand again and instructed the driver to hurry a little faster.

Throughout the evening, as people hugged and patted her, Shannon felt like she was living someone else's life. None of the chatter seemed significant to her. It was all about who was doing what and where they were going. There was no discussion of any relevance to her as a Christian. She could only imagine what Jesus would do in this room. That thought brought a smile to her lips.

"You look positively gorgeous," Armand said as he offered her a glass of sparkling water. "Everyone's thrilled you're back in town."

She smiled back at him and took a sip of her water. More than anything, she wanted the comfort of her friends who didn't care what she looked like.

"Armand?" she asked slowly.

At first, he didn't respond, but when she gently placed her hand on his shoulder, he turned to her. "Yes?"

"Do you ever think about eternity?"

He let out a nervous chuckle. "Not much. It's hard enough to worry about the here and now."

"I'm not talking about worry. I'm talking about. . ."

He winked. "I know where you're going with this. We can discuss our plans for the future when I get back."

She started to correct him and mention how her whole perspective had changed—how she now thought about her life in relation to her walk in the faith. But he'd already turned around and gotten into a conversation about the latest men's hairstyling product he was promoting. This obviously wasn't the time or place to discuss eternity with Jesus.

When Shannon began to yawn, Armand smiled. "I'm tired, too. We can leave in a few minutes if you want."

With a nod, Shannon replied, "That would be nice."

They were on their way to Shannon's building half an hour later. Armand walked her to the door, where the doorman pretended not to be listening.

"It's wonderful having you here with me, Shannon. I look forward to a long career and life together."

"But. . ."

He lifted a finger and held it to her lips to shush her. "I know, it's going to be hard being apart for the next several weeks, but it'll be good for both of us. We'll have time to think about the time ahead."

He left her with the doorman and got back into the limo before Shannon had a chance to respond. He lowered the window, blew her a kiss, and waved before the car sped off.

Once inside her apartment, she stepped out of her shoes, leaned against the wall, and rubbed her aching feet. It had been months since she'd worn high heels.

Shannon felt like talking to someone who understood. She glanced at the clock on the mantle and realized she'd have to wait until morning to call Janie, who was probably in bed, sound asleep by now.

After setting her clock and slipping into her nightclothes, Shannon reached for the Bible she'd brought to New York.

Settling under the covers, she opened to the book of Matthew, where she often found comfort. She read chapter nine over and over, taking to heart Jesus' healing power. He'd healed her physically and emotionally. Now she prayed that she'd be given the strength to do what she knew was right.

If she stayed in New York, she'd need to find a way to stay spiritually grounded. Janie would know what to do.

Shannon closed her Bible, turned off the light, and snuggled down under the covers. Light from the city filtered through her sheers, so the room wasn't completely dark. She watched the shadows dancing on the wall and listened to the sounds from the street below until her eyelids grew heavy.

The alarm woke her early, before the sun came up. She sat up, rubbed her eyes, and trudged to the kitchen, flipping lights on along the way.

When she was fairly certain Janie would be up and almost ready for the day, she reached for the phone in the kitchen and punched in Janie's number. She answered right away.

At first, Janie sounded excited to hear from her, but after Shannon asked for advice, her voice became cool and distant. "I can't tell you what to do, Shannon."

"I'm not asking you what to do. All I want is for you to pray for me."

"You didn't have to call to ask for that. I've been praying for you nearly all my life."

When Shannon hung up, she felt even worse than she had before she'd called. The rest of the day, all she could think about was Janie's attitude. It hurt.

After spending most of the day with Melinda and running a few errands, Shannon went back up to her apartment. No matter how hard she tried to resist calling Judd, she knew she had to hear his voice. He sounded thrilled to hear from her.

"Hey, how's it going?" he asked.

"Oh, pretty good. I did great on the test shoots."

"I knew you would. So, when will we see your mug on TV? Anytime soon?"

"I'm not sure. There's still a bunch of preliminary stuff that has to be done."

"You don't sound overjoyed."

"I'm not, Judd. In fact, I've been miserable since I've been here. I miss all of you so much, I'm thinking about coming back."

He let out a chuckle. "You haven't exactly given it much of a chance. It takes more time than a week or two to get back into the swing of things."

"But I loved the way things were in Atlanta. I miss the Bible study group. I miss you and Janie and Paul and. . ."

"Find a group up there. New York is a big place. I'm sure you can connect with a Christian Bible study if you ask around."

"Yeah, you're right," Shannon said as her heart fell. She didn't realize it when she first placed the call, but now she knew she'd been hoping he'd beg—or at least encourage—her to come back.

They chatted for a few minutes, until Judd said he had a parent-teacher conference in an hour and he really needed to go.

"Don't give up so quickly, Shannon," he said before they got off the phone. "And if you can't find a Bible study group, I'll ask Uncle Garrett if he knows someone. He has friends all over the world. I bet he can hook you up in no time."

"Thanks, Judd."

She dropped the phone back into the cradle and leaned back on her elbows. Everything seemed wrong to her.

Miserable, she figured she might as well find a way to entertain herself tonight and then, tomorrow, she'd look for a place to worship on Sunday. It wouldn't be easy, because none of her acquaintances in New York went to church. Sunday was their day to sleep in, when agents wouldn't bug them and clients spent time with their families and friends.

The first services Shannon attended were in a small church three blocks away from her apartment building. The preacher was an elderly gentleman whose bifocals kept falling off his nose. The man next to her kept nodding off to sleep, while the woman in the pew directly in front of her struggled to keep up with her two toddlers, who kept trying to climb over the back of the pew. Shannon had a very hard time concentrating on the message.

After church was over, she went up to the pastor and asked about singles' Bible study classes. Shaking his head, he said, "No, we haven't tried that here. I'm not sure how it would go over. Maybe. . ." He squinted as he adjusted his glasses again. "Do I know you from somewhere, Missy? You look awful familiar."

"No," Shannon replied, shaking her head and backing away. "I don't think so. Thanks for the good service, Pastor." Then she turned and ran out of the church before he figured out who she was and where he'd seen her.

The following Sunday, she went to a different church—this one a little bigger and a little closer to Greenwich Village. The crowd was younger, and the services were more contemporary. Maybe they'd have something similar to what her church in Atlanta had.

When the pastor asked everyone to turn to greet those around them, she shook the woman's hand behind her and asked if they had singles' Bible studies. The woman's eyes widened, she nudged the woman next to her, and they both squealed.

"I can't believe Shannon McNab is actually here!" the second woman said. That got everyone's attention, and before Shannon realized what had happened, she was signing everyone's church bulletin.

After church, all the people who hadn't been sitting close enough to get her autograph were thrusting pieces of paper and pens in her face, scrambling to get her signature. One man even asked her to pose for a picture with his teenage daughter. Shannon did it, then ran out as fast as she could to hail a taxi.

This wasn't working out. All she wanted was quiet worship on Sunday and a group to study the Bible with. Why was she having so much trouble in New York? It couldn't be that hard, could it?

Apparently so. The following Sunday was like a repeat of what had already happened. Shannon got to her apartment feeling like she'd been beaten in a very long race.

Armand was scheduled to return later on the next week. Melinda had a welcome-back party scheduled for the day after his arrival. She had always been good about celebrating every event in the lives of her superstars.

Doing as she was told, Shannon was there, waiting. She was one of the dozen people Melinda had invited to her office to greet Armand. He gasped, acting surprised, then crossed over to where Shannon stood. Placing his arm around her shoulders, he leaned over and whispered, "We need to talk."

Shannon nodded while Melinda grabbed him by the hand and pulled him off to the side to discuss some urgent business. She didn't keep him long, but it gave Shannon enough time to catch her breath before time to leave.

In the car, on the way to her place, Armand turned to her. "So how were things for you while I was gone?"

Shannon shrugged. "I went to a different church every Sunday."

He tilted his head back and howled, like she'd told him a

very funny joke. She didn't see the humor in the situation.

Dropping the smile, he said, "You don't need church, Shannon. Maybe you did after your accident, but things are all better now. You're modeling again."

Shannon sat there staring straight ahead as her thoughts tumbled over each other.

"Hey, what's wrong? Aren't you happy about how things are turning out? Isn't this what you wanted?"

"I'm not sure about modeling, but I do know one thing. I love the Lord, and I want to find a church where I can worship Him without feeling like I'm sitting in a fishbowl."

"That's silly," he said. "Your life was always good, long before you ever went to church. What did all those people in Atlanta tell you?"

She looked him in the eye. "Armand, I feel sorry for you. Without Jesus in your life, you're lost. Until I understood all He did to save people like us, I had no idea. But now I know, and I don't want to turn my back on my Savior."

Armand rubbed his hand over his mouth as he shook his head. Shannon sensed his discomfort, but she didn't say what she knew it would take to make him smile again. She couldn't lie to him and say she didn't need the Lord now that she had modeling back in her life. One was nothing but shallow, empty promises—an illusion—while the other was eternal and solid.

"Look, Shannon, why don't you go on inside and get some sleep? I'll come over in the morning with breakfast."

Nodding, Shannon hopped out of the car and scurried in past the doorman while Armand's car sped off. She sensed that things were about to come to a head between her and Armand.

The next morning, when Shannon got up, she put on some jogging pants and a T-shirt and didn't bother with makeup. All she did was brush her teeth and wash her face before running a brush thought her hair, letting it fall freely over her shoulders.

When she opened the door to Armand, he shuddered. "Go make yourself presentable, Shannon. This is so not like you."

"It is me, Armand. The real me."

"I've never seen this side of you."

"That's because you've never really looked, Armand."

"Your image—"

She cut him off. "I don't care about image—especially when I'm just hanging out around the apartment. Do you care how I look?"

He reached up and touched his perfectly styled hair and made a grimace. "I guess I do sort of care."

"Fine. Then find someone else who cares, because I don't."

Shannon was shocked at the words that had tumbled so easily from her mouth, but she felt free and relieved it was out. She really didn't care what he thought. And now he knew.

"You haven't been yourself lately. Maybe that accident was more traumatic than we realized."

"No, Armand. Now I am being myself. The way I was before the accident wasn't the real me." She gestured toward the kitchen. "I've got some tea ready. What'd you bring for breakfast?"

Shannon nibbled on the croissant and fruit Armand had brought, while he just sat there staring at the wall behind her. He clearly didn't want to look at her without makeup.

When he left, Shannon suspected she'd never see him again outside the agency, which was fine. He wasn't the right man for her anyway. This had been the second time he'd bolted when her image wasn't what he wanted. He only loved her when she was picture perfect. In other words, he loved her image and not the real Shannon McNab.

The man she truly loved was Judd. Shannon longed for things the way they were back in Atlanta. She had an urge to call Janie and talk, and if Janie acted cool and distant, she'd fuss at her until she loosened up.

"Whoa, Shannon, slow down," Janie said after Shannon rattled off all her feelings. "Let me see if I got this right. You don't like New York or modeling, and you don't ever want to see Armand again. You miss Atlanta and the church, and you're pretty sure you're in love with Judd."

"That's right," Shannon said firmly.

"Are you sure about this?"

"Positive."

"Okay, then I guess it's okay to tell you Judd's in love with you, too. He's been a wreck since you've been gone."

Shannon's heart fluttered before falling again. "Why doesn't he let me know?"

Janie laughed out loud. "You're not stupid, Shannon. It's pretty obvious. Here you are, a supermodel, bringing down more money in a year than he'll make in a lifetime. He's a school teacher in a small Atlanta suburb, and he's never even sure if his shoes match half the time."

"I don't care about all that."

"Maybe you don't, but he does."

"Judd has never cared if I wore makeup or not."

"He probably never even noticed," Janie agreed.

"And he was nice to me, even when my scar was bright red."

"We all have scars, Shannon. Judd knows that. It's just that some of us have scars on our faces, and others have them hidden inside."

"That's what I love about you, Janie."

"I know, I know. I don't beat around the bush."

"What should I do?"

"How would I know? I've never been faced with anything like this before."

"I don't know if I want to model anymore, but I do know

one thing. I don't want to stay here. I want to come back and be with my friends."

"If you come back here, you sure won't get those big modeling contracts you get up there."

"Maybe I can commute."

"Now that's a thought."

"Thanks, Janie."

"For what? Confusing you?"

Melinda called three hours later. "Are you feeling okay, Shannon?"

"Sure, I'm fine. How about you, Melinda?"

"Never mind me. Armand's worried about you."

"Tell him to relax. There's nothing wrong with me."

"Good," Melinda said, her voice tight with excitement. "Because I've got some wonderful news for you."

"You do?"

"We've just been offered a two-year extension on the corn chips contract, and I think we can renew the makeup contract before the week's over. Looks like you're really back, Shannon McNab."

Shannon's insides clenched as Melinda went over all the details. Dread washed over her with each statement and contract point. How would she ever get out of this?

"Well?" Melinda finally said. "Aren't you excited?"

ten

Shannon gulped. For most people, this would be the best news ever. But not for her. Not now, anyway.

"Can I get back with you on this, Melinda?"

"What are you talking about, Shannon? This is exactly what we were hoping would happen."

"Yes, I know, but. . ." Her voice trailed off. She wasn't yet sure how to handle this.

"Tell you what, Shannon. Come to my office first thing tomorrow morning. Maybe by then you'll be over the shock of all this good news. That'll give us time to have all the paperwork in."

Panic gripped her throat.

"Shannon?" Melinda said. "Are you still there?"

"Yes, I'm here. I'll see you in the morning."

The second Shannon got off the phone with Melinda, she dialed Pastor Manning's office back in Atlanta. He answered.

She started right in, talking ninety miles an hour, explaining everything, baring her deepest thoughts and feelings, including how much she cared for his nephew.

"I can tell you've been doing quite a bit of thinking," he said when she slowed down to catch a breath.

"What do you think about me commuting?"

"I have no idea how your business works, Shannon. You'll have to decide that."

"What would Judd say?" she said, her voice softer as she asked one of the hardest questions she'd ever asked.

"I'm not sure that matters. I do know he wants you to be

happy, though." He paused before asking, "Do you want to continue modeling?"

"I'm not sure."

"Maybe you'd better decide that before you take your next step. Just don't sign anything until you're positive you want to wrap years of your life around something so demanding."

"I'd like to ask one favor of you, Pastor."

"Sure, what's that?"

"Please don't discuss any of this with Judd. I'd like to be the one to bring it up."

"That goes without saying. I never reveal anyone's private conversation, even to LaRita. My family understands that about me."

"But I would like for you to tell Judd I've been thinking about him."

"He'll be glad to hear that, I'm sure."

"I don't know what I'd do without all of you," Shannon said as her eyes misted.

"You wouldn't have such a dilemma, would you?"

She laughed. "I guess not."

"Let's say a prayer, shall we?"

Shannon closed her eyes as Pastor Manning prayed for her wisdom in this monumental decision. He prayed for her continued healing and her witness to the people she came in contact with every day. "In your name, Jesus, amen."

"Amen," Shannon whispered before saying good-bye to Pastor Manning.

By the next morning, Shannon knew what she was going to do. There was no way she could give one hundred percent to her modeling career if she commuted from Atlanta. She had enough experience to know how grueling the assignments were, and putting herself through that would be too stressful and distracting from her faith. The Lord didn't intend for any of His followers to have more on their plates than they could handle.

There were plenty of hurdles she had to deal with now that she'd made up her mind. First of all, she needed to discuss this with Melinda, who would never understand. Shannon didn't expect to have an easy time of it, explaining how she'd chosen to walk away from a career Melinda had carefully crafted for her. Although Shannon was grateful, she had to be firm.

Armand would give a little resistance, but she knew his attention span was short. He'd argue for a little while, but he'd quickly get over her and move on to the next flavor of the month. What they had was a boatload of mutual professional respect—not love. She'd tell him that, and he might or might not understand.

The hardest person to talk to would be her mother. Not only had Sara McNab been known to be the proverbial stage mom, but her daughter was living her dream. Shannon knew she had to brace herself for some of the biggest guns her mother would pull out—quite likely the guilt speech about how she'd given up everything so Shannon could have the life she was so carelessly turning her back on.

Melinda greeted her the next morning, smiling and chipper. "Ready to sign for the next two years, Shannon? Things are looking up for you."

"Uh, Melinda, we need to talk."

Shannon gently guided Melinda back into the office, where she sat down and started explaining what she planned to do. Melinda's face turned pasty white, but she didn't utter a word until Shannon was finished.

"You're making the biggest mistake of your life, Shannon. These people were reluctant to take a chance on you. I had to twist a few arms to get these contracts."

"I know," Shannon replied. "And I appreciate what you've done, Melinda."

"You have no idea."

"You've been like a second mother to me."

Melinda stared a hole through her, making her feel like she'd committed some sort of sin.

"Do you want me to be miserable?" Shannon finally asked.

Rather than answer directly, Melinda stood from her chair, nodded toward the door, and said, "You may leave now, Shannon. And don't even try to make another comeback. I'll make sure you never get another decent contract again."

"Melinda," Shannon said. "I'm—"

"Good-bye, Shannon," Melinda said as she moved toward the door and grabbed the knob. "I'll deal with the clients. There's no need for you to contact anyone."

This was final. Shannon had never seen such a staunch expression on Melinda's face before. As she passed her agent, she turned and smiled, but Melinda didn't bother to acknowledge her. Once she'd gotten out the door, it shut so quickly, she could feel the breeze behind her.

Shannon went straight to her apartment and dialed Armand's cell phone number. He picked it up right away.

"What do you think you're doing, Shannon?" he bellowed.

"You know?"

"Yes, I know. Melinda called me right after you left her office."

"I want a life that's truly my own," Shannon replied. "I want to go back to Atlanta and have my old friends."

"You do realize we're finished, then, don't you?" he asked.

"Yes, Armand. I realized that a long time ago."

"Good-bye, Shannon."

When she hung up, she realized she could never turn back now. She'd closed some doors, walked the plank, and burned bridges. From now on, she'd have to free fall and land wherever the Lord put her. Every single cliché she'd ever heard about moving on with life entered her mind.

Suddenly, she burst into a fit of giggles. Nervous giggles. Shannon McNab was now a civilian—not the famous supermodel she once was. Sure, she still had some ads in print, and she'd see her commercials on television until they played out. But once they were over, that was it. She needed to look ahead and find a new purpose in life.

It was exhilarating but scary. She'd never done anything so drastic in her life.

Although she considered herself a strong woman, she hated the idea of hurting her mother, which she knew was inevitable. Now it was time to place the dreaded call to her parents.

She picked up the phone and started punching in the numbers, but before she pushed the last number, she hung up. No matter how much she needed to do this, she simply couldn't.

After several false starts, Shannon finally gave up and decided this was news best delivered in person. She called the airline and made reservations to Atlanta for the next day.

❧

Once she arrived in Atlanta and picked up her luggage, she headed straight for the first taxi she saw. After giving the driver directions, she settled back in her seat and shut her eyes. This would be difficult at best—maybe even the most emotional experience she'd ever have to deal with once her parents realized she'd completely shut the door on modeling.

"Thanks," she said as she paid the cab driver and pulled her bags from the trunk.

Standing at the curb for several seconds, Shannon shut her eyes and said a prayer for guidance and strength. Then she trudged forward.

The front door was unlocked when she turned the knob.

"Mom!" she hollered once inside the Williamsburg-style home.

Her mother suddenly appeared, her eyes wide, her face pasty white. "Shannon! What are you doing home? Has something happened?" She took Shannon by the arm and led her to the couch in the living room.

"I'm just fine, Mom. Nothing happened."

Shannon's dad came into the room and gave her a hug. "Good to see you, sweetie."

"Good to see you, too, Dad."

He let go and grinned at her. "I did all the repairs for that family in North Carolina. The man's wife was grateful, and she let me know his drinking problem had been turning their family upside down. She told me to thank you for being so understanding."

Shannon felt a lump in her throat and couldn't speak. She reached out and squeezed her father's hand.

"I thought you were back at work in New York," her mother said. "What are you doing here?"

Shannon cleared her throat and started slowly but managed to get the story out as her mother's eyes glistened with tears. She could tell she was ripping the heart out of the woman who'd sacrificed everything just so she could have the princess-style life of a supermodel.

"I just can't believe all this," her mother said. "You're throwing it all away."

"No, I'm not, Mom. I had a wonderful time modeling. Now I'm ready for something more challenging."

"What can be more challenging than what you were doing in New York?"

"I want to live the type of life that would be pleasing to Jesus."

"Don't tell me you've done all this for religion."

Shannon paused to carefully choose her words. Since her mother had never had a personal relationship with Jesus, she didn't understand what Shannon was talking about. To her mother, anything related to church was lumped into the category of "religion."

"It's not for religion," Shannon said slowly. "I just can't continue going through the motions of pretending to be something I'm not."

"But you're beautiful, and everyone wants to see your face in magazines and on TV."

"That's just an image, Mom."

Shannon watched her mother as everything sank in. They stood in silence as her mother's initial shock turned to grief then anger.

"Shannon McNab, what you've just done is as good as slapping me in the face."

"I'd never do that. I love you and Dad. I just want you to understand."

"Well, I don't understand, and I'm not sure I ever will."

Shannon's father remained silent, watching, his fingers steepled in front of him.

"Dad, do you understand?" Shannon asked. Until now, he'd never said a word about his feelings.

He started to nod before glancing at her mom. Then he took a step back before speaking. "Shannon, honey, I'm okay with whatever you want to do. If you're tired of modeling and need to be in Atlanta, for whatever reason, it doesn't matter; I'm glad to have you here. Life's too short to be unhappy."

"But—," her mother said before he silenced her with a stern look Shannon had never seen him use before.

"Shannon's a grown woman with plenty of money, Sara. She doesn't need anything from us. All she's asking for is understanding. I think we owe her that. She's been a model daughter, no pun intended, and I'm proud of her whether she's a model in New York or a churchgoing Atlanta girl."

"Thanks, Dad." Suddenly a thought occurred to Shannon. "Would you two like to go to church with me sometime?"

Her mother started shaking her head, but her father lifted both eyebrows. "We just might do that. If it's good enough to bring you all the way back to Atlanta, there must be something to it."

"That's not all that brought me back," Shannon admitted. "There's this guy. . ."

"But what about Armand?" her mom said between gasps.

"I'm not sure about Armand," Shannon told her.

"What's there not to be sure of? You and Armand were an item. Everyone knew the two of you were in love. You were the perfect couple."

"Not perfect," Shannon said. "And not in love. It was just the image of being in love."

"I don't know if you even know the meaning of love, Shannon. Armand was good to you. He looked at you with adoring eyes, and he took you to the nicest places."

"So he could be seen," Shannon explained.

"What does this other guy do for a living?" her mother asked.

"He teaches school."

"Very honorable profession," her father said. "And I see nothing wrong with our daughter dating a schoolteacher."

"But a teacher doesn't make nearly enough money to support our daughter in the style she's used to."

"Wait a minute," Shannon said, figuring it was time to interject her two cents. "Who said anything about him supporting me? All I said was that I liked him."

"You always have to think about these things," her mother told her. "Especially at your age."

"Give it up, Sara," her father told her. "Our daughter is smart. She can figure out what she wants. If she's tired of modeling and hanging out with her male-model friend, she's earned the right to come down here and be with anyone she wants."

Shannon offered her father a smile of gratitude. He didn't talk much, but when he did speak, his words meant something.

Her next surprise visit would be to church on Sunday. She hadn't let anyone know she'd be there. Hopefully, she'd find her friends to be as welcoming this time as they had been when she'd first met them.

Fortunately, she'd held on to her apartment, so she wouldn't have to stay with anyone. Her car had been at her parents' house, so she drove it home. When she got there, she pulled the curtains and blinds open, then started dusting. Since no one knew she was coming, the place hadn't been prepared. She liked the fact that she had something to do to keep her busy until Sunday.

After dusting and running the vacuum over the carpet, she took off for the grocery store to stock up on essentials, like bottled water, yogurt, veggies, fish, and chicken. And now that she didn't have to watch her figure quite as closely, she made a side trip down the ice cream aisle, grabbing her favorite flavor, creamy pistachio.

On Saturday, she had to resist the urge to call Janie. As much as she knew she could trust her best friend, she didn't want to take a chance on people finding out. She wanted everyone to know at the same time that she was back to stay. That way no one's feelings would get hurt.

Shannon was a lot more conscious of how she dressed Sunday morning. She didn't want to stand out, but she knew people would stare from shock. She chose navy slacks and a tan turtleneck. She brushed her hair to a glossy shine and let it flow freely over her shoulders. One quick glimpse in the mirror let her know she looked fresh, clean, and ready to face the people who mattered most to her.

❧

"Shannon!"

LaRita Manning was the first person to spot her when she pulled into the parking lot. Pulling her husband by the hand, LaRita came running, her arms open wide and ready for a hug.

"I'm so happy to see you! I thought you were still in New York. What brings you to Atlanta? Are you on location?"

Shannon smiled back, suddenly feeling shy. "No, I'm just here because I want to be here."

"Great reason for coming." She turned and hollered, "Hey, Judd, look who's here!"

Before Shannon could catch her breath, she found herself surrounded by all her friends from the Bible study—all except Janie. She glanced over her shoulder, then back to the group.

"Looking for someone?" she heard from the side.

"Janie!" Shannon ran over to her and lifted her off her feet.

"Put me down, Amazon Woman."

They both cracked up. It had been years since Shannon had heard Janie call her Amazon Woman, a name she'd used back in junior high school when Shannon shot up in height before anyone else. She stood a head taller than any guy in their grade until a few years later in high school.

When Judd approached, she noticed how a small smile twitched at the corners of his lips, but he never said a word. He just stood there, gazing at her as if he wasn't sure this was for real.

Shannon sat between Janie and Judd during church. It felt good to be sandwiched between two people she loved. After the services ended, Janie told her she wished she'd known she was visiting, or she wouldn't have made plans.

"That's okay," Shannon tried to assure her. "I'm not visiting. I'm here for good."

Janie offered a look of disbelief. "I'll call you later this week."

"I'm sorry, too," Judd said as he stood a few feet away, his hands thrust deep in his pockets. "I'm working with some kids in my class on the school play."

"Hey, don't worry about it," Shannon said. "Will you be at the Bible study tomorrow night?"

"Of course. I'm always there."

"Good. I'll see you then."

Judd nodded, but she could tell he was guarded. It was painfully obvious that no one believed she was here to stay.

"Can we ride to the Bible study together?" Shannon asked, feeling like it was time for boldness.

After a brief hesitation, Judd nodded. "I'll pick you up at six thirty."

She'd hoped he might offer to go to dinner first, but she figured this was better than nothing. "See you then."

❧

From the moment Shannon got in Judd's car to the time they arrived at the church, he talked about the kids at the school where he taught.

At first, Shannon listened with interest, but soon she realized he was using an evasion technique. He didn't want to talk about anything personal.

"Stop," she finally said when they pulled into the parking lot.

Resting his hand on top of the steering wheel, he turned to her. "This is my life, Shannon. I love what I do. Just like you love what you do." Being the perfect gentleman, he came around to her side of the car and held it as she got out, but he still hadn't warmed up to her.

"Thanks, Judd," she whispered. She hadn't corrected him or tried to explain anything. It was painfully evident words wouldn't change anything; she'd have to prove that she was here because she wanted a permanent change in her life. She wanted to live in a more Christ-centered way.

Shannon wasn't up on what they were studying, but now she knew she could sit back and listen. No one thought any worse of her for doing that, and she was comfortable with this knowledge.

She briefly reflected back on her first time at the Bible study. She'd felt like a fish out of water. Now she felt the connection between these followers of Christ. A warmth flooded her as she thought about the value of what she'd learned.

Once the study session was over, each person shared events from their lives since the last meeting. They prayed for each other, friends, and families. Then everyone turned to Shannon, waiting for an explanation.

Suddenly feeling put on the spot, Shannon lifted her shoulders, grinned, and said, "It's great to be back. I'll participate more next week, after I have a chance to catch up." She looked around at all the wide-eyed people and added, "I'm here to stay. I'm not kidding."

No one said anything. They just looked at each other before breaking for the evening. Shannon got the impression they didn't believe her about coming back.

Janie gave her a perfunctory hug before taking off. Shannon stood and stared after the friend she'd known longer than anyone else. This reception wasn't what she expected. No one was mean, but there was a distance she hadn't anticipated.

As she and Judd walked to his car, she turned to him. "Can we go somewhere and talk?"

"Sure, that's fine. Where?"

"How about the Dunk 'n Dine? I'm kind of in the mood for some of their fabulous pancakes."

"Your wish is my command," he said as he wriggled his eyebrows.

All the way to the restaurant, Judd told one anecdote after another, making her laugh. But she knew he was avoiding discussing anything with meaning. Had she caused this?

"I'll have the Monster Stack," Shannon said, pointing to the picture on the plastic menu.

"You said you were in the mood for pancakes, but I never expected this," Judd said as he leaned on his forearms. "Aren't you worried about watching your figure? I've always heard cameras add at least ten pounds."

"Haven't you been listening to me?" she countered. "I told you I'm here to stay. I'm not going back to New York. My modeling days are over. I want to stay here."

"But why?"

"Because this is real. What I had in New York was just a dream. One scar that doesn't go away, and the image is shattered."

"But your scar did go away. You can have your old life back."

Shannon groaned. "Sometimes, Judd Manning, you can be impossible."

He chuckled. "That's part of my charm."

"Yes, you're right," she agreed.

A serious look replaced his grin. "Okay, so let's say you do stick around. What then?"

"I don't know. Why don't we take it one day at a time?"

"You'll have to understand if it takes awhile for everyone to accept this as a reality," he said. "We care about you, but we don't want to have our hearts broken again."

Shannon understood. And he was right. She'd taken off at the first sign that she might be able to have her old career back. How could they ever believe she was serious about staying and this was what she really wanted after how she'd taken off so quickly?

Judd drove her home after they finished eating. As he walked her to her door, she reached out and took his hand. He didn't pull away, which was a good start. Shannon had to hold on to what little bit of hope she could find. When they reached her doorstep, Shannon hoped he might kiss her. But he didn't. He reached out, tweaked her nose, and then took a step back, almost as if he'd been burned.

"G'night, Shannon. See ya on Sunday."

With a heavy heart, she said, "Good night, Judd. Thanks for the ride."

Once inside her apartment, Shannon instantly headed for the phone. She called Janie.

"I gotta talk to you, Janie."

"It's late. Can we talk tomorrow?"

"Yeah. Come over after work. I'll cook dinner."

Janie sighed. "Okay, fine. See you then."

The next day seemed to drag, but finally, Janie's knock came at the door. Shannon had dinner cooked. She opened the door and directed Janie to the kitchen.

"I hope you're hungry. I cooked all your favorites."

Janie sniffed the air. "Pot roast? Mm. You must want something."

Sticking her fist on her hip, Shannon spun to face her best friend. "You think I'm up to something?"

"Of course I do. You're always up to something."

"You're right," Shannon conceded. "I'll tell you about it while we eat."

She explained how she'd come back for good and that she knew for sure she wasn't the slightest bit interested in going back to modeling. Janie ate and listened but didn't utter a word.

Finally, Shannon couldn't take it anymore. "Well? You haven't said what's on your mind. What are you thinking?"

Janie swallowed her food. "I don't know if you really want to know."

"Yes, I do want to know. This is important to me, Janie."

"Okay, but brace yourself. It's gonna hurt."

"I can take it."

"Everyone in the group really cares about you. Especially Judd. In fact, he's been moping around since you left. And when we saw that shot in 'Entertainment Tonight' with you leaving the award show with Armand at your side, I thought he'd fall over from grief."

"You watched the award show with Judd?"

"Yeah," Janie said. "The whole group got together because someone said you might be there. We were hoping to catch a glimpse of you. What we hadn't expected was seeing you hanging on Armand's arm."

A combination of dread and panic flooded Shannon. "That was all set up."

"Are you saying you didn't try to get back with Armand?"

"No, that wouldn't be true. But the old feeling I once had for Armand just wasn't there. It was all for publicity. My agent arranged for Armand and me to be seen together every chance she got."

"I don't know if Judd will believe that," Janie told her.

"He has to."

"You know, I feel sort of bad about this whole thing because I brought you to the group."

"You regret that?"

Janie put her fork down, pushed away from the table, and looked Shannon in the eye. "This is hard for me to say, Shannon, but I have to. We've known each other too long for me not to level with you."

"Just say it."

"When I saw you on TV, I felt like I'd been used. You needed someone after your accident. Then once you were all better, you ran back to New York. You didn't need us anymore."

"Used?" Shannon pointed to herself. "You think I used you?"

Shaking her head, Janie replied, "I don't know what to think. After listening to you now, I'm not sure."

That hurt more than anything Janie could have said. Shannon had never used anyone in her life. But then again, she couldn't blame Janie or any of the rest of them. At least she knew what she was up against now.

"I'll prove to you and everyone else I'm sincere," Shannon said as Janie stood at the door.

"You don't have to prove anything to us. Just remember, we have flaws, and we don't always see things for how they really are."

"How well I know." Shannon hugged Janie, then watched out the window as her friend walked to her car.

Early the next morning, after Shannon came in from her morning run, she showered, dressed, and headed for her parents' house. Maybe her mother would understand now.

"Shannon, I'm still not happy about this. You're giving up way too much to suit me."

"That's not why I came, Mom."

"I called Melinda earlier this week. I think she'll take you back if you call and tell her you had a brief spell of insanity."

"That's not what I want."

Sara leveled her with a glare. "Then you're making a huge mistake, and I'm afraid you're on your own this time. I can't keep fixing your problems, Shannon. Not when you intentionally sabotage your own career."

As Shannon left her parents' house, she felt more alone than at any other time in her life. Without her mother giving her support and Janie not completely trusting her, she felt like she had to go out on a limb without a safety net below.

Once back in her apartment, Shannon pulled the drapes, turned on a light, and pulled out her Bible. She shut her eyes and prayed for guidance and the ability to overcome all doubt from her friends. She wanted to let them know she was sincere. Now that she knew Christ, her entire perspective had changed.

Before she went to bed, she called Janie. "Please stop by in the morning."

Janie groaned. "You know I have to work in the morning."

"Then get up half an hour earlier, and I'll have coffee and a pastry for you."

"Okay, if it's that important to you."

"It is."

eleven

"I never thought I'd see this," Janie said as they sat sipping coffee the next morning in Shannon's apartment. "Especially after you went back to New York."

"Everything changed for me once the Lord came into my life."

"Yeah, that happened with me, too." Janie set her coffee mug down on the table. "I believe you now, Shannon, but you can't blame Judd for being guarded."

"I'll do whatever it takes."

"I guess you just have to give him time."

"That's all I can do."

After Janie left for work, Shannon straightened her apartment. All she could think about was what she and Janie had discussed. If only there were something she could do to make Judd believe her. She had a strong suspicion, verified by Janie, that he cared about her as much as she did him, but he was concerned about her commitment to the Lord, so he continued to guard his heart. She really couldn't blame him.

When the phone rang, she hoped it was Judd, but it wasn't. It was Melinda.

"I hate to bother you like this, Shannon," she said, her voice cool and emotionless, "but you still have to finish two of your contracts."

"I thought everything was complete."

"Everything except a couple of photo sessions and one commercial. As far as I can tell, that'll be it."

Shannon blew out a breath of frustration. She'd already given up her lease on the New York apartment, so she'd have to find a place to stay.

"Can you try to schedule it all together?"

"You know how hard that can be," Melinda replied. "I'll do my best."

"That's all I can ask. Thanks, Melinda."

"I'll let you know when you need to be here."

After she got off the phone, a weary feeling descended over her. Actually, it was more like dread. Just the thought of posing for magazine ads and shooting more commercials wore her out.

A couple of weeks went by, and she still hadn't heard from Melinda. Maybe she'd managed to get her out of the contract. If she didn't hear back in a few days, Shannon figured she'd call to make sure.

Her mother was still upset, but she tried not to let it affect her. She understood how much time, money, and energy her mother had put into her career, so she tried to be sensitive. Her father, on the other hand, seemed overjoyed to have her back in town. He'd pulled Shannon off to the side a few times and told her he thought she was making a wise decision.

In the meantime, she hadn't missed a single Bible study session. That was the one thing in her life in which she found total comfort. Jesus was constant—never changing. He loved her no matter what, and she never ceased to be amazed by the extent of His grace and mercy.

When Judd called and asked if she'd like to get together to prepare for the lesson, Shannon gave him a resounding "Yes!" After she hung up, she danced around her apartment, singing and praising the Lord. Maybe things were looking up between them!

The next day, Shannon got up, went shopping, and came home to get the apartment ready. She wanted it squeaky clean and neat. She even baked cookies.

He walked in and sniffed the air, his expression warm and tender. "Did you bake something?"

Shyness overcame her ability to speak. This had never happened to her before, so she wasn't sure how to react. As she nodded, a smile found its way to her lips. He grinned right back at her.

"You're amazing, Shannon."

"You're pretty amazing yourself, Judd." Her voice barely came out in a whisper, so she cleared her throat. "Would you like a cookie?"

"Of course."

She scurried to the kitchen, then brought out a plate of cookies. His eyes widened.

"You baked those?"

"All by myself with these two hands."

"Is there anything you can't do?"

Shannon let out a nervous laugh. She was used to praise from her fans, but this was different. This was coming from Judd.

He led the study session. As they went through all the questions in the workbook, Shannon felt his gaze as it lingered on her long after she responded. After they finished the lesson, he closed the book and placed it on the table.

"Shannon, I guess you've probably noticed I've been acting sort of weird lately."

"Well, yeah, I have noticed. What can I do?"

He shook his head. "It's me. I'm dealing with some issues."

"I understand," she said. He obviously didn't want to talk about it. Maybe she needed to give him a little space to make up his mind to talk to her about his feelings. And she also needed to pray about the relationship. What she wanted and what the Lord had in mind for her might be two entirely different things.

❧

That week's group Bible study went extremely well. She and Judd contributed more than most of the others, which gave her a great feeling because they'd been so far behind in the beginning.

As they were gathering their things to leave, Janie came up to her and gave her a hug. "I'm so happy to see you deeply immersed in the Word."

Shannon hugged her back. "Thanks for leading me here."

"It wasn't me." Pointing her finger upward, Janie reminded her, "He did it all. I'm just the vehicle."

❧

Judd watched Shannon as she animatedly chatted with Janie. Every time he looked at her, his heart rate increased. And when she looked back at him, he felt like he could jump over the moon. It wasn't just infatuation, either. He was in love.

When he'd first met Shannon McNab, his reaction was the same as any other male. Her beauty stunned him. With the exception of the scar from her accident, she seemed perfect. If anything, her beauty was a turnoff to him. He was so far from perfect, he didn't want any part of a relationship with a woman who'd make all his flaws more obvious. Then, as he got to know her, he'd learned some of her imperfections, and that was when he started falling in love. As confident as Shannon seemed, he knew she had some insecurities. That made him love her even more, and he wanted to protect her. He'd also learned that her modeling career hadn't been her idea. She was living her mother's dream, something else that endeared her to him. She wanted her mother to be happy—even going so far as to center her whole life around it.

But the one thing that excited him most was, just as his own faith had begun to grow, he was able to witness the same thing happening to Shannon. Her love for the Lord was evident on her face and in every action. She was truly dedicated and loyal to her faith.

When she'd gone off to New York after her scar had healed, he had to face the possibility that he'd only been a temporary distraction for her while she was healing. Her return had surprised him. At first, hope welled inside him that possibly she was here to stay. But what if she left again and he had to go through the emptiness he'd felt the first time she'd gone? Could he deal with that?

Janie had tried to talk to him, saying Shannon was sick of modeling. He heard her words, but he didn't want to take them to heart.

What if she was right? Did he dare take a chance and allow the love he felt for Shannon to show?

All his life, Judd had wanted the security of a stable home and being surrounded by people who knew him and loved him no matter what. He'd resorted to being the class clown in school, which helped him as a teacher. He knew what made children tick, and he could handle those kids who acted out for attention because he'd once been one of them. His knack for working with children and his love for reading and the English language had earned him a dream position in an excellent school. His aunt and uncle had provided him with a roof over his head while he saved money for a down payment on a house. And through his uncle, he'd found a fabulous group of friends he knew had good hearts and the desire to live in a way that was pleasing to Christ. What more could a man ask for?

The only thing Judd could think of was a woman to spend the rest of his life with. To his dismay, he'd been mentally putting Shannon in that role, although he knew his chances with someone like her had to be slim.

Over the past week, Janie had encouraged him to pursue

his feelings for Shannon. Did he dare?

After long hours and days of worrying about it, he decided to just go for it. What did he have to lose? It wasn't as if he hadn't been defeated before.

With a sigh, Judd resigned himself to having to face another disappointment. He could do it. He had enough practice.

Armed with prayer and the desire to follow his dream regardless of the consequences, Judd headed for church on Sunday hoping to have a chat with Shannon immediately afterward. The only problem was, she wasn't there. He craned his neck and looked over the sea of heads around him, but he couldn't find Shannon in the entire congregation. Janie smiled and waved as their gazes met. She'd know where Shannon was. He'd just ask her after church.

The sermon seemed to be directed at him, as always. Even the worship songs got to him. When his uncle dismissed the congregation, he said a silent prayer, then jumped up to find out where Shannon was.

Janie shook her head. "Sorry, Judd. She had to take off for New York yesterday afternoon. Her agent called and ordered her back."

He gulped hard, the lump in his throat nearly choking him. "She went back to New York?"

Offering a look of sympathy, Janie nodded. "Sorry, Judd." She reached out and touched his arm. "I wish my news were different."

"Hey, don't worry about it. At least we can all watch her on TV, right?"

Several people from the Bible study group joined them, and Janie quickly started chatting with one of the other women. Judd turned down an offer to go out to lunch. He'd much rather go on home. Besides, he had an appointment with his Realtor in a couple of hours. He'd been looking at houses, and he was ready to get serious about buying his first home.

❧

"I'm giving you one last chance," Melinda said as she stood in front of her desk. "If you want to sign, I think I can save the contracts."

"No, Melinda, but thanks. I really don't want to do this anymore."

"How does your mother feel about this?"

"You know how she feels. This is what she's always wanted for me."

For the first time since she'd met Melinda, something happened. Melinda came toward her, draped her arm over Shannon's shoulder, and pulled her to her side. "Ya know, Shannon, I really don't think your heart was ever into modeling. This was your mother's dream, and she was able to live it through you. If you want to live in Atlanta and do something else, I don't think anyone should stand in your way."

Tears instantly sprang to Shannon's eyes. "Thanks. I appreciate that."

"Keep in touch, okay, honey?"

Unable to speak, Shannon nodded and left. Now it was time to go to the hotel, gather her things, and get on the next plane home to Atlanta. She had a whole life ahead of her.

She got back just in time to freshen up and get to the Bible study, where she hoped to see Judd. Janie looked shocked that she was there.

"I thought you left again."

"I just had to finish out a contract."

"Uh-oh." Janie covered her mouth with her hand.

"What?" Shannon reached for Janie's hand and pulled it away. "What happened?"

"Judd—"

"Say no more."

Before anyone could stop her, Shannon ran out the door, hopped into her car, and drove straight to Pastor Manning's house. LaRita answered the door.

"Come in, Shannon," she said in her usual sweet voice. "What a nice surprise. Garrett, Shannon's here."

Pastor Manning came around the corner, his hand extended. "How's the modeling business?"

"I wouldn't know. I quit."

He frowned. "I thought you went back to New York." He paused, raised his eyebrows, and added, "Again."

"I think I have a few things to explain. Where's Judd?"

"He isn't living here anymore."

Shannon gasped. "What happened?"

LaRita led Shannon to a loveseat, then sat down next to her. Patting her on the leg, she said, "Judd found a nice house close to the school where he teaches. He moved out last weekend."

"Oh," Shannon said as relief flooded her. "I need to talk to him."

"Let me call him over," Pastor Manning said as he grabbed the phone and started punching numbers.

Shannon listened to the phone conversation and heard Pastor Manning's firm tone, insisting Judd come over right away. There was some arguing, but it wasn't too serious.

"He's as stubborn as his uncle," Pastor Manning said as he hung up. "He'll be here in about twenty minutes."

"I've got cake and coffee in the kitchen," LaRita said. "Want me to bring you some?"

"I'd like that," Shannon replied. She'd always loved the warmth of the Manning's home. It felt inviting—like a place a person could totally relax. She now realized this was something she'd missed growing up.

Shannon explained what had happened with her modeling contract. They listened attentively and told her they understood and respected what she'd done. That meant quite a bit to her.

When Judd arrived, LaRita turned to her husband and said, "Let's leave them alone. Why don't we go on to bed now?"

Judd stood with his hands in his pockets, his jaw set in determination. Shannon rose and walked toward him, but he didn't budge.

"Please sit down, Judd. We need to talk."

"I don't have anything to say."

She expelled a sigh. "Look, I know how stubborn you can be, but I'm just as stubborn—maybe even more so. You might as well listen now, or I'll never give you any peace."

She looked at his face as it softened somewhat. Finally, he nodded and walked over to the chair where his uncle had been sitting.

"I just got back from New York this afternoon, and I went to the Bible study, hoping to see you there."

"I moved."

"Yes, I heard. That's great. Congratulations. Would you like to tell me about your house?"

He darted a glance at her, then looked away before he stood up and started pacing. "Look, Shannon, I don't know what kind of game you're playing, but I don't like it. You come and you go, back and forth, whenever the mood strikes. This isn't how I want to live my life."

"I understand," she said.

"I don't think you do. I'm going to tell you something that might rock your boat a little, but I feel like I need to be honest with you. I've tried hard not to, but I think I might have fallen in love with you. It's not something I should admit, I know, but it's the truth. If I let you continue to waltz in and out of my life like this, I'll wind up a crazy man."

As Shannon listened to his profession of love for her, she

felt like her heart might explode. It took every ounce of self-restraint she had to hold back her announcement of love for him. He needed to get this off his chest.

He stopped for a few seconds, grimaced, then resumed pacing. "What's more, I bought a house, deluding myself into thinking you might consider becoming my wife. I have no idea what I was thinking. What would a woman like you want with a man like me?"

As he wound down, Shannon sat there with her hands in her lap, joy slowly rippling through her, then flooding her like a tidal wave. It took every ounce of self-restraint she had to keep from jumping up and flinging her arms around him. Finally, when he stopped, she ordered him to sit.

"Finished?" she asked.

He nodded. "Yeah."

"Okay, my turn. I'll have you know, Judd Manning, that I've been in love with you for a long time. I was wondering the same thing you were. What would a man who had his act together want with a woman like me? After all, I was never sure what I wanted to do with my life. I figured you'd want someone with her feet planted firmly on the ground."

She dared to take a look at him. He'd raised his eyebrows, and he was watching her with interest. She knew she needed to make this good, or she'd blow what could be her only chance to convince him of her love.

"All my life I dreamed of finding peace, contentment, and a little happiness," she said, carefully choosing her words. "When I met you, I found it all rolled into one masculine bundle. I love you, Judd."

"But what about your modeling?"

"I quit."

"You went back, though."

"I had to finish out a contract. Now it's all over. I'm here to stay."

Taking one of the biggest chances ever, she reached out and touched his hand. *Please, Lord, don't let me lose this man.*

Slowly, he turned his hand over and wrapped his fingers around her hand. Shannon felt the tug as he pulled her to his side. Their gazes held until their faces were inches apart.

He lifted both hands and cupped her face. "Shannon, I love you. I tried my best not to let it happen, but it was impossible."

The feeling was so overwhelming, the urge so strong, Shannon couldn't resist reaching out and pulling his face to hers. She lightly brushed his lips with her lips before backing away so she could look him in the eye.

"I've loved you since the first time you kissed me," she whispered.

"Really? Me, too."

Shannon's heart pounded as she held her breath and wondered what to do next.

Suddenly, Judd sucked in a breath, blew it out, and said, "Shannon McNab, will you mar—"

The words weren't even all the way out of his mouth when she shouted, "Yes!" Then, an odd feeling overtook her. What if she'd mistaken what he was saying? "Uh, what were you about to ask, Judd?"

He chuckled. "I was about to ask if you'd be my wife."

"That's a relief." She kissed him again then pulled back. "I'd be honored to be your wife."

Applause sounded from the hallway before Garrett and LaRita appeared. "Good move, nephew."

Judd cast a warning glance toward his aunt and uncle. "Eavesdropping?"

"Of course," LaRita replied. "But only after we heard

Shannon shout, 'Yes!' We wanted to make sure you didn't blow it."

"Well? How'd I do?"

"Magnificently," Pastor Manning replied. "And Shannon didn't do too badly, either."

LaRita motioned for everyone to join her in the kitchen. "Cake and coffee for all."

Shannon laughed. "You've already fed me cake. I'm gonna get fat."

Judd nudged her. "Who cares? You've caught your man."

"In that case, I'd love some cake."

On the way to the kitchen, Shannon pinched herself to make sure she wasn't dreaming. Then she said a silent prayer. *Thanks, Lord, for making my dream come true. Amen.*

A Letter To Our Readers

Dear Reader:

In order that we might better contribute to your reading enjoyment, we would appreciate your taking a few minutes to respond to the following questions. We welcome your comments and read each form and letter we receive. When completed, please return to the following:

Fiction Editor
Heartsong Presents
PO Box 719
Uhrichsville, Ohio 44683

1. Did you enjoy reading *Love's Image* by Debby Mayne?
   ❑ Very much! I would like to see more books by this author!
   ❑ Moderately. I would have enjoyed it more if

   ____

   ____

   ____

2. Are you a member of **Heartsong Presents**? ❑ Yes ❑ No
   If no, where did you purchase this book?______________

   ____

3. How would you rate, on a scale from 1 (poor) to 5 (superior), the cover design? ______________

4. On a scale from 1 (poor) to 10 (superior), please rate the following elements.

   ____ Heroine
   ____ Hero
   ____ Setting
   ____ Plot
   ____ Inspirational theme
   ____ Secondary characters

5. These characters were special because?______________________

____

____

6. How has this book inspired your life?______________________

____

____

7. What settings would you like to see covered in future **Heartsong Presents** books? ______________________________

____

____

8. What are some inspirational themes you would like to see treated in future books? ______________________________

____

____

9. Would you be interested in reading other **Heartsong Presents** titles? ❑ Yes ❑ No

10. Please check your age range:

❑ Under 18	❑ 18-24
❑ 25-34	❑ 35-45
❑ 46-55	❑ Over 55

Name ____

Occupation ____

Address ____

City____________________ State________ Zip____________

ALABAMA

4 stories in 1

Nestled in the northeastern mountains of Alabama is the fictional town of Rockdale. The small Southern town has become a haven for four women who have given up on finding love.

Four complete inspirational romance stories by author Kay Cornelius.

Contemporary, paperback, 480 pages, 5 3/16" x 8"

Please send me ____ copies of *Alabama*. I am enclosing $6.97 for each. (Please add $2.00 to cover postage and handling per order. OH add 7% tax.)

Send check or money order, no cash or C.O.D.s please.

Name ______________________________

Address ______________________________

City, State, Zip ______________________________

To place a credit card order, call 1-800-847-8270.

Send to: Heartsong Presents Reader Service, PO Box 721, Uhrichsville, OH 44683